The Sisterhood
Book One

WEEKEND WARRIORS

A Selection of Recent Titles by Fern Michaels
from Severn House

ANNIE'S RAINBOW

CAPTIVE EMBRACES

CAPTIVE INNOCENCE

CAPTIVE SECRETS

DEAR EMILY

FUTURE SCROLLS

PICTURE PERFECT

SARA'S SONG

SINS OF THE FLESH

SINS OF OMISSION

SPLIT SECOND

TENDER WARRIOR

TEXAS FURY

TO TASTE THE WINE

VALENTINA

VIXEN IN VELVET

Prologue

Washington, DC
January, 1998

The traffic was horrendous on Massachusetts Avenue but then it was always horrendous at this time of day. Rush hour. God, how she hated those words. Especially today. She slapped the palm of her hand on the horn and muttered under her breath, 'C'mon you jerk, move!'

'Take it easy, Nik,' Barbara Rutledge said, her eyes on the slow moving traffic. 'One more block and we're there. Mom won't mind if we're a few minutes late. She hates it that she turned sixty today so the longer she has to wait for the celebration, the better she'll feel. I don't think she looks sixty, do you, Nik?'

'Are you kidding! She looks better than we do and we're only thirty-six.' She leaned on the horn again even though it was an exercise in futility. 'Just tell me one thing, why did your mother pick the Jockey Club for dinner?'

'The first crab cakes of the season, that's why. President Regan made this restaurant famous and all her political friends go here. If you want my opinion, thirty bucks for two crab cakes is obscene. I can eat lunch all week on thirty bucks if I'm careful. Mom pitched a fit last week when I took her to Taco Bell for lunch. We both ate for five bucks. She was a good sport about it but she can't understand why I don't tap into the trust fund. I keep

1

telling her I want to make it on my own. Some days she understands, some days she doesn't. I know she's proud of me, you, too, Nik. She tells everyone about her two crime fighting girls who are lawyers.'

Nikki looked at her seat companion, the girl she'd called sister from sandbox days. She was so pretty with short brown hair that curled in a pixie cut. Her eyes were the color of the sea on a stormy day and she had the most beautiful smile in the world. To make her even more perfect, she had a personality that attracted everyone to her within seconds of meeting her. 'I love her as much as you do, Barb. I can't imagine growing up without a mother. I would have if she hadn't stepped in and took over when my parents died. OK, we're here and we're only thirty minutes late. This isn't the best parking spot in the world but it will have to do and we're under a street light. In this city it doesn't get any better than that.'

'We really should hit the powder room before we head for the table. Mom does like spit and polish, not to mention perfume and lipstick,' Barbara said, trying to smooth the wrinkles out of her suit. Nik did the same thing.

'I spent the day in court and so did you. We're supposed to look wrinkled, messy and harried. Myra will understand. Ooops, almost forgot my present,' Nik said reaching into the back seat for a small silver-wrapped package. She handed Barbara a long cylinder tied with a bright red ribbon. 'Your brain must be as tired as mine. You almost forgot yours, too. What about this pile of books, Barb?'

'They're for Mom. I picked them up today at lunch time. You know how she loves reading about murder and mayhem. I'll give them to her when we leave.'

Myra Rutledge was waiting, a beautiful woman whose

smile and open arms welcomed them. 'My girls are here. We're ready to be seated now, Franklin,' Myra said.

'Certainly, Madam. Your usual table or would you prefer the smoking section with a window view?'

'The window, Franklin,' Barbara said. 'I think tonight in honor of my mother's birthday, you two can have a cigarette. Just one cigarette after dinner for both of you. I will, of course, abstain. Yes, yes, yes, I know we all quit but this is Mom's birthday and I say why not.'

Myra smiled as she reached for her daughter's hand. 'Why not, indeed.'

'This is so wonderful,' Myra said sitting down and leaning across the table. 'My two favorite girls. I couldn't ask for a better finale to my birthday.'

'Finale, Mom! Does that mean when you go home, you and Charles won't celebrate?'

'Well . . . I . . . perhaps a glass of sherry. I did ask Charles to come but he said this was a mother–daughter dinner and he would feel out of place. No comments, girls.'

'Mom, when are you going to marry the guy? You've been together for twenty years. Maybe even longer for all I know. Nik and I know all about the birds and the bees so stop blushing,' Barbara teased.

'Yes and it was Charles who told you two about the birds and the bees,' Myra smiled.

Charles Martin was Myra's companion slash house-man. When his cover was blown as an MI6 agent, his government had relocated him to the United States where he'd signed on as head of security for Myra's Fortune 500 candy business. His sole goal in life was to take care of Myra and her company – a job he took seriously and did well. Both girls were grateful for his attention to

3

Myra, lessening her loneliness when they went off on their own.

Myra's eyes sparkled. 'Now, tell me everything. Your latest cases, who you're dating at the moment, how our softball team is doing. Don't leave anything out. Will I be planning a wedding anytime soon?'

It was what Nikki loved about Myra the most, her genuine interest in their lives. She'd never invaded their privacy, always content to stand on the sidelines, offer motherly support and aid when needed but never interfered, or gave advice unless asked. Nikki knew Myra enjoyed the times the three of them spent together, loved the twice monthly dinners in town and the occasional lunches with her daughter or perhaps a short stroll along the Tidal Basin.

Yes, Myra had a life, a busy life, a life of her own beyond her girls. She sat on various charitable boards, worked tirelessly for both political parties, did numerous good deeds every day, was active in the Historical Society and still managed to have time for Charles, Barbara and herself.

'You staying in town tonight, Mom?'

A rosy hue marched across Myra's face. 'No, Barbara, I'm going home. No, I didn't drive myself. I took a car service so don't fret about the trip to McLean. Charles is waiting for me. I told you, we'll have a glass of sherry together.'

'No birthday cake!' Nik said.

The rosy hue crept down to Myra's neck. 'We had the cake at lunch time. Charles needed a blow torch to light all the candles. All sixty of them. It was very . . . festive.'

'How does it feel to be sixty, Mom?' Barbara asked

reaching for her mother's hand across the table. 'You told me you were dreading the day.'

'It's just a number, just a day. I don't feel any different than I did yesterday. People always talk about "the moments" in their lives. The special times they never forget. I guess this day is one of those moments. The day I married your father was a special moment. The day you were born was an extra special moment, the day Nikki came to us was another special moment and then of course when the candy company went 500. Don't laugh at me now when I tell you the other special moment was when Charles said he would take care of me for the rest of my life. All wonderful moments. I hope I have years and years of special moments. If you would get married and give me a grandchild I would run up the flag, Barbara. I don't want to be so old I dodder when you give birth.'

Nikki poked Barbara's arm, a huge smile on her face. 'Go on, tell her. Make your mother happy on her sixtieth birthday.'

'I'm pregnant, Mom. You can start planning the wedding, but you better make it quick or I'll be showing before you know it.'

Myra looked first at Nikki to see if they were teasing her or not. Nikki's head bobbed up and down. 'I'm going to be the maid of honor and the godmother! She's not teasing, Myra.'

'Oh, honey. Are you happy? Of course you are. All I have to do is look at you. Oh, there is so much to do. You want the reception at home in the garden, right?'

'Absolutely, Mom. I want to be married in the living room. I want to slide down the bannister in my wedding gown. I'm going to do that, Mom. Nik will be right behind me. If I can't do that, the wedding is off.'

'Anything you want, honey. Anything. You have made me the happiest woman in the whole world. Promise that you will allow Charles and me to babysit.'

'She promised me first,' Nikki grinned.

'This is definitely "a moment." Do either of you have a camera?'

'Mom, a camera is not something I carry around in my purse. However, all is not lost. Nik has one in her car. I'll scoot over there and get it.'

Nikki fished in her pocket and tossed her the keys.

'I'm going to be a mother. Me! Do you believe it? You'll be Auntie Nik,' Barbara said bending over to tweak Nikki's cheek. 'I'll ask Franklin to take our picture when I get back. See ya,' she said flashing them both an ear to ear grin.

'I hope you had a good day today, Myra. Birthdays are always special,' Nikki said, her gaze on the window opposite her chair. 'Knowing you're going to be a grandmother has to be the most wonderful thing in the world. I'm pretty excited myself.' She could see Barbara running across the street, her jacket flapping in the spring breeze. 'Do you remember the time Barbara and I made you a birthday cake out of cornflakes, crackers and pancake syrup?'

'I'll never forget it. I don't think the cook ever forgot it either. I did eat it, though.'

Nikki laughed. 'Yes you did.' She was glad now she had parked under the street light. She could see several couples walking down the street, saw Barbara open the back door of the car, saw her reach for the camera, saw her sling it over her shoulder, saw her lock the door. She turned her attention to Myra who was also staring out the window. Nikki's gaze swivelled back to the window to see Barbara look both ways for oncoming traffic, ready to sprint across the street at the first break. The three couples were almost upon her when she stepped off the curb.

Nikki was aware of the dark car that came out of nowhere, the sound of horns blowing and the sudden screech of brakes. Myra was moving off her seat almost in slow motion, her face a mask of disbelief as they both ran out of the restaurant. The scream when it came was so tortured, so animallike; Nikki stopped in her tracks to reach for Myra's arm.

The awkward position of her friend's body was a picture that would stay with Nikki forever. She bent down, afraid to touch her friend, the friend she called sister. 'Did anyone call an ambulance?' she shouted.

She heard a loud jittery response: 'Yes.'

'No! No! No!' Myra screamed over and over as she dropped to the ground to cradle her daughter's body in her arms. From somewhere off in the distance a siren could be heard. Nikki's trembling fingers fumbled for a pulse. Her whole body started to shake when she couldn't find even a faint beat. Maybe she wasn't doing it right. She pressed harder with her third and fourth fingers the way she'd seen nurses do. A wave of dizziness rivered through her just as the ambulance crew hit the ground running. Tears burned her eyes as she watched the paramedics check Barbara's vital signs.

Time lost all meaning as the medical crew did what they were trained to do. A young woman with long curly hair raised her head to look straight at Nikki. Her eyes were sad when she shook her head.

It couldn't be. She wanted to shout, to scream, to stamp her feet. Instead, she knuckled her eyes and stifled her sobs.

7

'She'll be all right, won't she, Nikki? Broken bones heal. She was just knocked unconscious. Tell me she'll be all right. Please, tell me that. Please, Nikki,' Myra pleaded.

The lump in Nikki's throat was so large she thought she would choke. She tried not to look at the still body, tried not to see them straighten out Barbara's arms and legs. When they lifted her on to the stretcher, she closed her eyes. She thought she would lose it when the young woman with the long curly hair pulled a sheet up over her best friend's face. Not Barbara. Not her best friend in the whole world. Not the girl she'd played with in a sandbox, went to kindergarten with. Not the girl she'd gone through high school, college and law school with. She was going to be her maid of honor, babysit her baby. How could she be dead? 'I saw her look both ways before she stepped off the curb. She had a clear path to cross the street,' she mumbled.

'Nikki, should we ride in the ambulance with Barbara? Will they let us?' Myra asked tearfully.

She doesn't know. She doesn't know what the sheet means. How was she going to tell Myra her daughter was dead?

The ambulance doors closed. It drove off. The siren silent.

'It's too late. They left. You'll have to drive, Nikki. They'll need all sorts of information when they admit her to the hospital. I want to be there. Barbara needs to know I'm there. She needs to know her mother is there. Can we go now, Nikki?' Myra pleaded.

'Ma'am?'

'Yes, officer,' Nikki said. She loosened her hold on Myra's shoulders.

His voice was not unkind. He was too young to be this kind. She could see the compassion on his face.

'I need to take a statement. You are . . . ?'

'Nicole Quinn. This is Myra Rutledge. She's the mother . . .' She almost said: of the deceased, but bit her tongue in time.

'Officer, can we do this later?' Myra interjected. 'I have to get to the hospital. There will be so much paperwork to take care of. Do you know which hospital they took my daughter to? Was it George Washington University Hospital or Georgetown Hospital?' Myra begged. Tears rolled down her wrinkled cheeks.

Nikki looked away. She knew she was being cowardly but there was just no way she could get the words past her lips to tell Myra her only daughter was dead. She watched as police officers dispersed the crowd of onlookers until only the three couples remained. Where was the car that hit Nikki? Did they take it away already? Where was the driver? She wanted to voice the questions aloud but remained silent because of Myra.

Nikki watched as the young officer steeled himself for what he had to do. He worked his thin neck around the starched collar of his shirt, cleared his throat once and then again. 'Ma'am, your daughter was taken to the morgue at George Washington Hospital. There's no hurry for the paperwork. I can have one of the officers take you to the hospital, if you like. I'm . . . I'm sorry for your loss, ma'am.'

Myra's scream was primal as she slipped to the ground. The young cop dropped to his knees. 'I thought she knew. I didn't . . . Jesus . . .'

'We need to get her to a doctor right away. Will you stay with her for a minute, officer? I need to get my cell phone out of the car to make some calls.' Her first call was to Myra's doctor and then she called Charles. Both promised to meet her at the emergency entrance to GW Hospital.

When she returned, Myra was sitting up, supported by the young officer. She looked dazed and her speech was incoherent. 'She doesn't weigh much. I can carry her easily to the squad car.'

Nikki nodded gratefully. 'Can you tell me what happened, officer? Did you get the car that hit Barbara? Those couples standing over there must have seen everything. We even saw it from the restaurant window. Did they get the license plate number? I saw a dark car but it came out of nowhere. She had a clear path to cross the street. He must have peeled away from the curb at ninety miles an hour.'

'I ran the license plate one of the couples gave us, but it isn't going to do any good.'

'Why is that?' Nikki rubbed at her temples as a hammer pounded away inside her head.

'Because it was a diplomat's car. That means the driver has diplomatic immunity, ma'am.'

Nikki's knees buckled. The young cop reached out to steady her.

'That means he can't be prosecuted,' Nikki said in a choked voice.

'Yes, ma'am, that's exactly what it means.'

One

Sixteen months later

It was dusk when Nikki Quinn stopped her BMW in front of the massive iron gates. She pressed the remote control attached to the visor and waited for the lumbering gates to slide open. She knew Charles was watching her on the closed-circuit television screen. The security was sophisticated, high-tech, impregnable. The only thing missing was concertina wire along the top of the electrified fence.

Nikki sailed up the half mile of cobblestones to the driveway that led around to the back of the McLean mansion. When she was younger, she and Barbara had referred to the house as Myra's Fortress. She'd loved growing up here, loved riding across the fields on Barbara's horse Starlite, loved playing with Barbara in the tunnels underneath the old house that had once been used to aid runaway slaves.

The engine idling, Nikki made no move to get out of the car. She hated coming here these days, hated seeing the empty shell her beloved Myra had turned into. All the life, all the spark had gone out of her. She sat in the living room, drinking tea, staring at old photo albums, the television tuned to CNN twenty-four hours a day. She hadn't left the house once since Barbara's funeral. Nikki finally turned off the engine, gathered her briefcase, weekend bag and purse. Should she put the top up or leave it down? The sky was clear. She shrugged. If it looked like rain, Charles would put the top up.

'Any change?' she asked walking into the kitchen.

Charles shook his head before he hugged her. 'She's gone downhill even more these last two weeks. I hate saying this but I don't think she even noticed you weren't here.'

Nikki flinched. 'I couldn't get here, Charles. I had to wait for a court verdict. I must have called a hundred times,' Nikki said tossing her gear on the counter top. Her eyes pleaded with Myra's houseman for understanding.

Charles Martin was a tall man with faded blue eyes and a shock of white hair that was thick and full. Once he'd been heavier but this past year had taken a toll on him, too. She noticed the tremor in his hand when he handed her a cup of coffee.

'Is she at least talking, Charles?'

'She responds if I ask her a direct question. Earlier in the week she fired me. She said she didn't need me anymore.'

'My God!' Nikki sat down at the old oak table with the claw feet. Myra said the table was over 300 years old and hand hewn. As a child, she'd loved eating in the kitchen. Loved sitting at the table drinking cold milk and eating fat sugar cookies. She looked around. There didn't seem to be much life in the kitchen these days. The plants didn't seem as green, the summer dishes were still in the pantry, the winter placemats were still on the table. Even the braided winter rugs were still on the old pine floors. In the spring, Myra always changed them. She blinked. 'This kitchen looks like an institution kitchen, Charles. The house is too quiet. Doesn't Myra play her music anymore?'

'No. She doesn't do anything anymore. I tried to get her to go for a walk today. She told me to get out of her face. I have to fight with her to take a shower. I'm at my wit's end. I don't know what to do anymore. This is no way to live, Nikki.'

'Maybe it's time for some tough love. Let me see if she responds to me this evening. By the way, what's for dinner?'

'Rack of lamb, those little red potatoes you like and fresh garden peas. I made a blackberry cobbler just for you. But when you're not here, I end up throwing it all away. Myra nibbled on a piece of toast today.' Charles threw his hands in the air and stomped over to the stove to open the oven door.

Nikki sighed. She straightened her shoulders before she marched into the living room where Myra was sitting on the sofa. She bent down to kiss the wrinkled cheek. 'Did you miss me, Myra?'

'Nikki! It's nice to see you. Of course, I missed you. Sit down, honey. Tell me how you are. Is the law firm doing nicely? Are you still seeing that District Attorney?' Her voice trailed off to nothing as she stared at the television set whose sound was on mute.

Nikki sat down and reached for the remote control. 'I hope you don't mind if I switch to the local station. I want to see the news.' She turned the volume up slightly.

'Let's see. Yes, I'm still seeing Jack and the firm is doing wonderfully. We have more cases than we can handle. I'm fine but I worry about you, Myra. Charles is worried about you, too.'

'I fired Charles.'

'I know but he's still here. He has nowhere to go, Myra. You have to snap out of this depression. I can arrange

some counseling sessions for you. You need a medical
checkup. You have to let it go, Myra. You can't bring
Barbara back. I can't stand seeing you like this. Barbara
wouldn't approve of the way you're grieving. She always
said life is for the living.'

'I never heard her say any such thing. I can't let it go.
She's with me every minute of every day. There's nothing
to live for. The bastard who killed my daughter robbed my
life as well. He's out there somewhere living a good life.
If I could just get my hands on him for five minutes, I
would . . .'

'Myra, he's back in his own country. Shhh, listen. That
man,' Nikki said pointing to the screen, 'was set free today
because of a technicality. He killed a young girl and he's
walking free. Jack prosecuted the case and lost.'

'He must not be a very good District Attorney if he lost
the case,' Myra snapped. Nikki's eyebrows shot upward.
Was that a spark of interest? Childishly, she crossed her
fingers.

'He's an excellent District Attorney, Myra, but the law
is the law. The judge let things go because they weren't
legal. Oh, look, there's the mother of the girl. God, I feel
so sorry for her. She was in court every single day. The
papers said she never took her eyes off the accused, not
even for a minute. The reporters marveled at the woman's
steadfast intensity. Every day they did an article about her.
Jack said she fainted when the verdict came in.'

'I know just how she feels,' Myra said leaning forward
to see the screen better. 'What's she doing, Nikki? Look,
there's Jack!'

Nikki watched as the scene played out in front of her.
She saw Jack's lips move, knew he was saying something
but she couldn't hear over the voice of the excited news

reporter. She saw his arm reach out but he was too late. Marie Lewellen fired the gun in her hand point blank at the man who killed her daughter.

The television screen turned black and then came to life again. Barnes looked directly into the camera, his eyes wide with shocked disbelief. Blood bubbled from his mouth. 'I . . . should have . . . killed . . . you, too . . . you bitch!'

'You killed my little girl. You don't deserve to live. I'm glad I killed you. Glad!' Marie Lewellen screamed.

Barnes fell face forward on to the concrete steps of the courthouse.

Chaos erupted but the camera stayed positioned, capturing the ensuing panic.

'Oh my God!' was all Nikki could say.

Myra reared back against the cushions. 'Did you see that! That's what I should have done! I hope she killed the son of a bitch! Is he moving? I can't see. Is he dead, Nikki? Charles, come see this. Why didn't I have the guts to do what that woman just did?' Myra shouted, her skinny arms flailing up and down. 'If she killed him, I want you to defend her, Nikki. I'll pay for everything. Use your whole firm. Every expert, every specialist in the world. She killed him. She got in his face and killed him. Tell me he's dead. I want to know if he's dead!'

Nikki looked at Charles who was busy staring at the ceiling. 'He's dead, Myra.'

'Look, look! They're handcuffing her. They're going to take her to jail. I want you to leave right now. Post her bail, do something. Don't let them keep her in jail. Say you'll take her home with you. Tell them she won't be a menace to society. Charles, get my checkbook.'

'Myra, for God's sake, simmer down. It's not that easy.'

'The hell it isn't. She was crazed. Temporary insanity. Are you going to do it or not?'

'Yes, but . . .'

'Don't give me buts. You're still sitting here. I never asked you to do a thing for me, Nikki. Never once. I'm asking you now.'

'I didn't say I wouldn't do it, Myra. I need to think. I need to talk to Jack. I can have my paralegal go down to the station. Tomorrow morning will be time enough. There is no way in hell she's getting out of jail tonight. She has to be arraigned. Can you wait for morning, Myra?'

'Yes, I can wait for morning.' Myra swung around. 'Charles, did you see what that woman just did? I would cheerfully rot in prison if I had the guts to do that. First thing in the morning, Nikki. I want you to call me with a full report.'

'You don't answer the phone, Myra,' Nikki said sourly.

'I'll answer it tomorrow. Isn't it time for dinner? Let's eat off trays this evening. I want to see what happens to that poor woman. They'll be reporting on this for hours. Does she have other children? A husband? Isn't anyone going to answer me?'

Nikki's jaw dropped. Charles spun around on his heel, a smirk on his face.

'I can tell you what Jack told me. She has two other children, and yes, she has a husband. She's a homemaker. She works at a Hallmark shop on weekends for extra money that goes for all the little extras young kids need. Her husband is a lineman for AT&T. Her two boys are nine and eleven. Jenny, the daughter that was killed, worked after school till closing at the same Hallmark shop. She had a flat tire the night she was killed. She was fixing it herself when that creep offered to help and then he snatched her and dumped her body out near Manassas. Jack said they're a very nice family. Marie went to PTA meetings and they went to church as a family on Sunday.'

'They'll need someone to take care of the boys, to cook and do all the things a mother does in case they don't let her out right away. Charles, find someone for the family. Use that employment agency we use when we do our spring cleaning. I hope they give her a medal. Someone should.'

'Myra, for God's sake, she killed a man in cold blood. She took the law into her own hands. Civilized people don't do things like that. That's why we have laws.'

'Where was the law when that bastard killed my daughter? Did Barbara get justice? No, she did not! My daughter is dead and no one paid for that crime. My unborn grandchild is dead and no one paid for that crime either. Don't talk to me about justice. Don't talk to me about the law because I don't want to hear it. Those laws, the justice that freed that man . . . *suck*.'

Nikki looked up to see Charles standing in the doorway. She watched as both his clenched fists shot upward. In spite of herself she grinned. Myra was alive and belching fire. All she had to do was get her to calm down and maybe, just maybe, she would return to the land of the living.

It was midnight when Jack Emery finally returned Nikki's call. She crawled into bed, her head buzzing with the evening's events.

17

'Did you see it, Nikki?'

'Of course I saw it. Myra and Charles saw it, too. I'll say one thing, it snapped Myra out of her fugue. At least for now. She wants me to defend Marie Lewellen. I said I would.'

'You can't defend her. It's open and shut. Insanity isn't going to hold up. She admitted to buying the gun at lunch time from some punk on the street. That goes to premeditation. They've charged her with first degree murder. I'll be prosecuting, Nikki.'

'Pass on it, Jack. You did enough to that woman.'

'What the hell is that supposed to mean, Nikki?'

'It means that asshole got off. That's exactly what it means, Jack. Myra was right when she said it sucked. You didn't fight hard enough. He was guilty as sin and you damn well know it.'

'The judge threw out . . . Why am I defending myself? I did the best job I could under the circumstances. I tried to stop her at the courthouse. I was seconds too late. Don't go sour on me now. Turn it over to someone else in your firm, Nikki.'

'I can't do that, Jack. I promised Myra. She's never, ever, asked anything of me. I have to do what she wants. I'm going to give you the fight of your life, too.'

'If you take this case on that means we aren't going to be able to see one another until it's over at which point we'll probably hate each other's guts. Is that what you want?'

Nikki's mind raced. No, it wasn't what she wanted but she knew where her loyalties lay. She loved Jack Emery. 'Beg off, Jack. Let some other DA take the case?'

'I guess I'll see you in court, counselor,' Jack said coldly.

It was his tone not his words that sparked her reply. 'You bet your sweet ass you'll see me in court.' Nikki snapped her cell phone shut and threw it across the room. Nikki punched at the thick downy pillows. She knew she wasn't going to be able to sleep now. She felt like crying. A second later she bounded out of the twin bed and ripped down the covers from the bed that once belonged to Barbara. If she wanted to, she could stick her hand under the pillow and pull out Barb's old beat-up teddy bear and hug it to her chest the way Barb had done every night she slept in the bed. It almost seemed sacrilegious to touch it. Instead she picked up the pillow and looked down at the tattered bear named Willie. She almost stuck her finger in the hole under Willie's chin but changed her mind. She lowered the pillow and went back to her own bed. Tears rolled down her cheeks. 'God, I miss you, Barb. I think about you every day. I just had a fight with Jack. At least I think it was a fight. I wish you were here so I could call you up and tell you all about it.' She punched at the down pillows again. Maybe she needed to read herself to sleep. Her gaze traveled to the built-in bookshelves across the room. The three top shelves were hers because she was taller than Barbara. The three bottom shelves belonged to Barbara and were loaded with everything but books. No, she was too wired up to read.

The first month she'd come here to live, Myra had knocked out two walls and turned this room into a two-girl bedroom. They'd spent so many hours in here, huddled in their beds, giggling, telling secrets, talking about boys and sharing all their hopes and dreams. Even the bathroom had twin vanities, twin showers, twin toilets. Myra didn't stint and she didn't favor one over the other. She simply had enough love for both of them. She looked now at the twin desks, the colorful swivel chairs, the bright red rocking chairs. It seemed so long ago, almost like a lifetime. She stared at the colorful rockers and at the cushions they'd made at camp one year. Barbara's was perfect, her stitches small and neat; her own was sloppy, the seams loose. But it wasn't the cushions that held her gaze. The chair was rocking, moving slowly back and forth. She looked up to see if the fan was on. A chill washed down her spine. She shuddered as she reached for her robe. Maybe Charles had left some coffee in the pot. If not, she could make some more.

Nikki walked down the long hallway to the back staircase that led to the kitchen. She blinked when she saw Myra and Charles sitting at the table, highball glasses in their hands. She blinked again. 'I couldn't sleep,' she mumbled.

'We couldn't either,' Myra said.

'After what we saw on television this evening, I can understand why. I'm going to make some coffee.'

'Nikki, Charles and I want to talk to you about something.'

Nikki reached for the coffee canister. There was an edge to Myra's voice. A combative edge. Something she'd never heard before. 'About what, Myra? I said I would take Marie Lewellen's case.'

'I know. That's just a small part of it. Do you remember a while back when you told Charles and myself about two young women who came to see you? Kathryn Lucas and Alexis Thorne, only that wasn't Alexis Thorne's real name at the time.'

'I remember,' Nikki said measuring coffee into the stainless steel basket.

'You helped Alexis by going outside the law. You couldn't help Kathryn because the statute of limitations had run out, but if there was a way to help her, would you do it?'

Nikki felt herself freeze. 'Are you talking about inside the law or outside the law, Myra?'

'Don't answer my question with a question. Would you help her?'

'I can't, Myra. There's nothing I can do for her. I looked at everything. Time ran out. Yes, I feel sorry for her. I understand how it all went down. She waited too long, that's the bottom line.'

'You looked the other way for Alexis. You knew someone who was on the other side of the law and you got her a new identity, you helped her start a small home business as a personal shopper and you made it happen for her. You believed in her when she told you her story. She was a victim, she didn't deserve to go to prison for a whole year. She can never get that year of her life back. The men who turned her into a scapegoat walked free and are living the good life and her life is ruined. Kathryn is a victim and no one is helping her. Marie Lewellen could spend the rest of her life in jail unless you can get her off. Legally.'

Nikki sat down across from Myra and Charles. 'I think this would be a real good time for you to tell me *exactly* what you two are talking about.'

'The system you work under doesn't always work,' Charles said.

'Sometimes that's true,' Nikki said carefully. 'For the most part it works.'

Myra looked at Nikki over the rim of her glass. 'What if we take the part that doesn't work and make it work?

What if I told you I was willing to use my entire fortune – and you know, Nikki, that it is sizeable – and use it to . . . make that system work. For us. For all the Maries, the Kathryns and the Alexis Thornes who got lost in the system.'

'Are you talking about going outside the law to . . . to . . . avenge these women? Are you talking about taking the law into your own hands and . . . and . . .'

Myra's head bobbed up and down. 'Charles can help. He dealt with criminals and terrorists during his stint at MI6. You're an attorney, a law professor. With your brains, Charles's expertise and my money we could right quite a few wrongs. It would have to be secret, of course.'

'And you just now came up with all this?' Nikki said in awe. 'No!'

'Yes,' Myra and Charles said in unison.

Nikki looked at her watch. 'Just eight hours ago, give or take a few minutes, you were practically comatose, Myra. You didn't want to live. You were so deep in your misery and your depression I wanted to cry for you. Now you're all set to take on the judicial system and dispense your own brand of justice. You'll get caught, Myra. You're too old to go to jail. They aren't kind to old people in jail. *No!*'

Myra took a long pull from the highball glass. 'If I can't satisfy my own vengeance, maybe I can do something for others that the system failed.' She spoke in a low, even monotone. 'Kathryn Lucas, age 38. Married to Alan Lucas, the love of her life. Alan had multiple sclerosis and lived in a wheelchair. They owned an eighteen-wheeler, Alan's dream. In order to keep his dream alive for him, Kathryn drove the rig and Alan

22

rode alongside her. One night when they stopped for food and gas, Kathryn is raped at a truck stop by three bikers. Alan is forced to watch and cannot help his wife. Rather than report the rape and destroy what's left of her husband's manhood, she remains silent. She does nothing. She carries it with her day and night for the next seven years until Alan dies. Needless to say, whatever was left of the marriage after the rape died right then and there. The day after she buries her husband, she goes to you, gives you all the information she has on the case and you turn her away because the stupid statute of limitations has run out. You told me she had a partial license plate, that one of the bikers was riding an old Indian motorcycle. You said she told you they were called Weekend Warriors, probably white-collar professionals out for a fling. Charles said there aren't many Indians in existence and they're on every biker's wish list. It shouldn't be hard to track it down. You just sit there, Nikki, and think about three men raping you while Jack is forced to watch. You think about that.'

'Myra, I don't have to think about it. I feel terrible for Kathryn Lucas. Yes, she deserves to have something done, but she waited too long. The law is the law. I'm a goddamn lawyer. I can't break the law I swore to uphold.'

'The circumstances have to be brought into consideration. I need you to help us, Nikki.'

'What is it you want me to do?'

'We could form this little club. You certainly know plenty of women who have slipped through the cracks. Like Alexis, Kathryn and many others. We'll invite them to join and then we'll do whatever has to be done.'

Nikki stood up and threw her hands in the air. 'You want us to be *vigilantes!*'

'Yes, dear. Thank you. I couldn't think of the right word. Don't you remember those movies with Charles Bronson?'

'He got caught, Myra.'

'But they let him go in the end.'

'It was a damn movie, Myra. Make-believe. You want us to do the same thing for real. Just out of curiosity, supposing we were able to find the men that raped Kathryn Lucas, what would we do to them?'

Myra smiled. 'That would be up to Kathryn now, wouldn't it?'

'I don't believe I'm sitting here listening to you two hatch this . . . this . . . What the hell is it, Myra?'

'A secret society of women who do what has to be done to make things right.'

'It could work, Nikki, as long as we hold to the secrecy part,' Charles said quietly. 'There is that room in the tunnels where you and Barbara used to play. You could hold your meetings there. No one would ever know. I know exactly how to set it all up.'

Nikki struggled for a comeback that would make sense. In the end she said, 'Jack Emery will be prosecuting Marie Lewellen. We'll be adversaries.'

'I see,' Myra said. She slapped her palms on the old scarred table top. 'Then you have to get her out on bail and we'll find a way to whisk her and her family away to safety. I have the money to do that. It will be like the Witness Protection Program. Charles can handle all that.'

Nikki sat down with a thump. 'If I don't agree to . . . go along with this, what will you do?'

Myra borrowed a line from her favorite comedian. '"Then we'll have to kill you,"' she said cheerfully. 'So, are you in?'

'God help me, I'm in.'

Two

L ightning ripped through the darkness, a crazy quilt of fireworks in the sky. Thunder boomed at Mach 1 as the worst storm in five decades slaughtered the state of Virginia. Vicious waterfalls of rain reduced visibility, forcing the procession of vehicles to a halt.

The lead car's brake lights came to life as the driver waited for the electronic gates to swing open. In mid-swing, an arthritic limb from one of the three hundred-year old oaks crashed downward to land on top of the electrified fence of Myra Rutledge's McLean, Virginia estate.

The occupants of the cars shivered as the limb sizzled and crackled, flames shooting upward to meet the savage lightning attacking the night.

One by one, the cars proceeded to inch forward only to stop when the lead car sounded its horn and ground to a halt because the opening wasn't large enough to drive through. Doors swung open, rain-clad figures huddled, arms waving, their shouts carried away on the gusty, hurricane-like winds.

A piercing whistle – the kind heard at ball games – shrilled in the stormy air. 'Back up one at a time. Give me enough room and I'll take down the gates,' a voice ordered with authority.

With visibility at zero minus, the occupants of the cars

27

did their best to follow the order. Bumpers and front ends collided as a blast from the last vehicle in the procession of cars came to life with a savage bellow.

The eighteen-wheeler, driven by Kathryn Lucas, skirted the cars with long years of expertise. With a mighty roar that matched the rolling thunder overhead, she crashed through the massive iron gates. 'God, I always wanted to do something like that,' she chortled gleefully. 'Oh, Alan, I wish you could see what I just did. If it wasn't for this big rig, we'd all still be sitting outside those monster gates. Can you just see that ancient Rolls or the Benz tapping those gates! I swear those gates are made of something beside iron. I wouldn't be surprised if I did some serious damage to this fine vehicle. I love you, will always love you. Remember that, Alan. This is Big Sis signing off.'

Talking to her late husband always made her feel better. Believing her husband was still with her in spirit gave her great comfort. It didn't mean she was nuts, or that she was losing it. All it meant was she felt better and she was sharing her thoughts with the only man she ever loved or would love in the future.

The portico, as well as the old farmhouse, was awash with light, beckoning warmth and safety to the drivers of the vehicles. The Honda Civic, the customized Jag, the BMW and the Benz, lined up in formation and parked two across. The ancient Bentley parked behind the eighteen-wheeler.

Umbrellas were raised only to sail upward in the sixty-mile-an-hour winds. The five women sprinted toward the light spilling from the main doorway that was being held open by a tall, stately looking woman, Myra Rutledge. Rain poured through the open doorway, soaking the beautiful heart of pine floor. 'Welcome to Pinewood,' she said.

Charles Martin used all his shoulder power to shove the monster bolt into the lock position on the solid oak door. The bolt, the lock and the door itself dated back to the days when the slaves were routed through Pinewood to the underground railroad.

'Come, come. We have dry clothes for you all,' Myra said as she handed out thick, luxurious towels that were as large as bath sheets, along with a flat, white box containing candles.

'The power will probably go off soon, and there seems to be something wrong with the generator that lights this part of the house, so we're going to be using candle light until we can get the power working. Take any room at the top of the steps. Follow me, please,' Charles said.

The moment the women were out of sight, Myra lowered her body to the third step from the bottom of the breathtaking circular staircase. Her gnarled hand reached out to touch one of the polished oak spindles. She remembered all the times her daughter had whooped her way down the bannister, Nikki right behind her. They had both continued to do it for many years. It was all so long ago. Two years since that fateful day when her daughter had been killed. An eternity. Tears gathered in her eyes. She wiped at them angrily.

Now, it was payback time.

Myra looked around the foyer that was half as large as the church she worshiped in. There was no life here, no indication anyone truly lived here. Suddenly, she wished for flowers, huge bouquets of colorful Shasta daisies, green plants, cacti, anything to take away the museum-like look of the house. Flowers these past two years hadn't been a priority.

The chandelier overhead flickered, thanks to the rickety old generator. A moment later the only light to be seen came from the candle in Myra's hand. She wished now she had listened to Charles and replaced the generator, but in the scheme of things, generators hadn't been a top priority in her life these past two years either. She'd been too busy grieving, living in a cocoon of pure hell.

'We're coming down, Myra,' Nikki shouted from the top of the stairs. 'Hold the candle high!'

Myra thought she heard a giggle from one of the women and then, in the blink of an eye, Kathryn Lucas was whooping her pleasure as she slid down the polished bannister, her candle straight in front of her, Nikki behind her. Long years of practice allowed Myra to reach out one long arm to break the younger woman's fall. Nikki slid expertly to the floor and was on her feet a second later, a wide smile on her face.

'Now, that was fun! If I had a staircase like this, I'd be sliding down it morning, noon and night. Did you ever slide down, Mrs Rutledge?' Kathryn asked.

'Call me Myra. I did it once on the day of my fiftieth birthday. I wanted to do something outrageous, something silly. I was sore for a week, since there was no one at the bottom to catch me.'

'You know what I always say . . . I say whatever turns you on. Maybe someday I'll tell you about some of the way-out things Alan and . . . Never mind. That's a whole other story and a lifetime ago.'

Myra smiled. She liked this rambunctious young woman.

'Ladies, if you're dry and comfortable, I would like you to follow me,' Charles said. When the tight procession reached a solid wall of bookshelves, Myra stepped in front of Charles. With a trembling hand, she counted down the various carvings on the intricate molding that ran the length of the bookshelves. At the same moment her fingers touched the lowest carving, the wall moved slowly and silently to reveal a large room with wall-to-wall computers that blinked and flashed as well as a mind-boggling, eye-level closed-circuit television screen showing Kathryn's rig crashing through the electronic gates. Each wall seemed to be made up of television screens. MSNBC was playing on the south wall, CNN on the north wall. From somewhere, fans whirred softly, and there wasn't a window to be seen.

'This,' Myra said waving her arms about, 'is our command center and we have Charles to thank for insisting on putting in a cutting-edge, solar powered, electrical system. In spite of our current weather, there's enough stored power to last a month.

'Years ago, we installed a modern-day ventilation system when my girls used to play here. It's been updated recently. At one time, this was just a storage area with a trapdoor. This is where my ancestors took the slaves and routed them to safety. Beneath the house is a maze of tunnels. Charles and I hung bells at each entrance and exit so the girls wouldn't get lost. The tunnels have all been shored up by Charles in case . . . in case . . . we ever need to use them. Please, take your seats,' Myra said indicating a large round table surrounded by deep comfortable chairs. On the table, in front of each chair lay a bright, blue folder.

Kathryn Lucas whirled and twirled around as she looked at everything, the engineer in her appreciating what she was seeing. 'It looks like a war room,' she said, excitement ringing in her voice.

Myra smiled. 'That's exactly what it is. When you go to war you need a war room. Please, take your seats.'

Myra stood up, the palms of her hands flat on the table top. She looked at each woman in turn. She'd rehearsed a pat little speech, but suddenly she couldn't remember the words. Barbara had always said, 'Cut to the chase, Mom, spit it out.'

'You all know why you were invited here,' she began, her voice shaky. 'You all agreed to the rules as Nikki outlined them to you. All of you here this evening are victims of a justice system that doesn't always work. We can't save the world and we can't right the wrongs done to us, but we can avenge ourselves. I see us as sisters under the skin, a sort of sisterhood, if you will.'

'I like the way that sounds,' Kathryn said, settling back in her chair.

Myra paused to take a deep breath, to marshal her courage, to pray to God she was doing the right thing. 'Two years ago my daughter Barbara was struck down and killed by a hit-and-run driver, who had diplomatic immunity.' Tears welled in her eyes as her gaze swept the room. 'I want the man who killed her to pay for what he did.' She swallowed hard and then continued. 'I know each of you here tonight has suffered a loss that also went unpunished. We'll go over each case momentarily. Afterwards, we will pick a case for our immediate attention. As I point to you, please give us your name and your profession.'

'Isabelle Flanders, architect.'

'Alexis Thorne, securities broker. Actually, I'm an ex-securities broker and a felon. I am also a personal shopper.'

'Julia Webster, plastic surgeon.'

'Kathryn Lucas. I'm a cross-country truck driver. I'm also an engineer.'

'Yoko Akia. My husband and I own a flower shop.'

'Of course, you all know Nikki Quinn,' Myra said. 'Nikki spent several years with the FBI before opening her own law firm. She also teaches law at Georgetown University.' Myra held out her hands to Charles. 'Last but certainly not least, Charles Martin, my right hand and my left hand. Charles has many special talents as you will find out. To protect ourselves from each other, should any of you decide to expose our accomplishments, Charles will videotape each of our meetings.' She squeezed Charles's hand. 'If you will open your folders, we can get started.'

And God help us all, she thought.

'Inside each of your folders you will find your own case history and the case history of your sisters. We felt that it was necessary for each of you to get to know one another. However, reading about someone doesn't quite give you the same feel as seeing that person go about their daily routine. The stills and videos you are about to see were taken to help your sisters know you better. Please refrain from commenting until Charles turns off the screen. I'm sure you're all going to be a little surprised at what you see,' she said as the first picture appeared on the screen . . .

Nikki in a courtroom standing before a jury. 'We've been working on this presentation for some time now so there is quite a bit of footage even though it has been carefully edited.' The picture switched to Yoko working in her flower shop.

Hearing Yoko gasp, Myra said, 'Yes, we've been spying on all of you. We wanted to make an impression on you here tonight, to show how technologically capable we are and to show you that we mean to insure the secrecy of this organization.'

The women stared, transfixed as their images flashed across the screen. When the screen turned dark, twenty-seven minutes later, Kathryn Lucas was the first to speak. 'I don't see how videotaping me in my flowered underwear will help anyone get to know me better or insure the secrecy of the Sisterhood.'

'How did you get in my house?' Julia Webster demanded.

'You filmed me buying *Tampax*,' Alexis Thorne grumbled.

'You actually watched me buying groceries and saw that humiliating moment when I didn't have enough money to pay for them at the checkout?' Isabelle Flanders said angrily.

'It is no one's business but mine that I mix manure with peat moss for my plants,' Yoko Akia said quietly, her eyes lowered.

Nikki Quinn's eyes apologized and accused at the same time. 'I can't believe you videotaped me, Myra. Me, Myra. Christ, I'm the one who agreed to help you form the group! So what if I cried and kicked the door and threw the whole damn case file down the courthouse steps. So what, Myra. I hate to lose. I hate it when scumbags win and the good guys have no other recourse but to cry. I didn't see you or Charles on that damn film, Myra.' Her voice was so vehement, the other women sat up straighter in their chairs.

'It was done to remind you of why you're here, Nikki.' There was no apology in Myra's voice. 'It's to show you what we can do, what we're going to be doing from here on out. Think of it as your security blanket.' Nikki wasn't about to give up. 'There's more, isn't there?'

'Miles and miles of tape. It's all safe and secure. None of you have a thing to worry about since it's for your own protection. Yes, we were intrusive and yes, we were thorough. The reason Charles and myself aren't on the tape is because we're old and we're boring. And . . . we're paying for this party. End of discussion.'

The women looked at one another, but no one offered up a comment.

Myra picked up a red folder. Her movements were slow and deliberate. The women leaned forward expectantly.

'Alexis Thorne, you're here because the brokerage firm you worked for pinned a crime on you that they themselves committed. You did a year in prison for *their* crime. They ruined your life and you are now a felon with a new identity, thanks to Nikki Quinn.

'Isabelle Flanders, you're here because one of your trusted employees, while driving you to a construction site, had a car accident that killed a family of three. Because you were unconscious when they pulled you out of the wreckage, she accused you of driving the vehicle. You lost your business in the lawsuits that followed and you were wiped out financially. You are virtually living hand to mouth working at whatever you can find to support yourself while your employee will never have to work another day in her life thanks to generous court settlements.

'Julia Webster, you're here because you thought you

were married to a man who took his marriage vows seriously. He infected you with the HIV virus and made it impossible for you to continue your career as a plastic surgeon. A death sentence looms on your horizons because of those infidelities.

'Yoko Akia, you are here because your father brought your mother to this country under false pretenses. Unable to speak English at the time, she thought she was coming to the golden world. Instead of the golden world she expected, her world turned into a life of corruption and prostitution. She died at the age of 33.

'Nikki Quinn, you are here as our legal counsel. It's important for all of you to know that Nikki has put her career on the line to join us.'

Charles took that moment to press a button on the remote in his hand. Nikki's picture flashed on the monitor. The same picture that had appeared a short while ago. She flinched at the memory.

'Last but not least, sisters. I'm here because my daughter was killed by a hit-and-run motorist who had diplomatic immunity. At the moment there is nothing I can do but the day will come, I'm sure, when the man will find his way back to this country. When that happens, I want to be ready to exact my vengeance. Until that happens, I'm here to help you in whatever way I can.

'What we're going to do now is this. Each of you write your name on the slip of paper that Charles will give you and drop it into the shoebox in the middle of the table. Charles will pick a name and that's the first case we'll work on.'

Myra watched the play of emotion on the women's faces as they wrote their names on the small squares of paper Charles handed out. She saw misery, despair, hope and hatred. She couldn't help but wonder whose name would come out of the box.

Charles clicked the remote and a statue of the Scales of Justice flashed on the monitor. This was Myra's cue to end her speech. 'Unlike her,' she said pointing to the screen, 'we are not blind, nor do we care about the scales of justice because those scales favor the criminal more than the victim.'

'Kathryn Lucas,' Charles said clearly, reading from the slip of paper he'd drawn from the Keds shoebox.

Kathryn swallowed hard as the others stared at her. She felt light-headed. She turned to look around the room. She saw everything as in slow motion. It was all so surreal. 'I have to get my dog out of the truck. I didn't think we'd be here this long. I don't know why I left him in the truck. I shouldn't have done that. It's like . . . like when I left Alan in the truck that . . . that time. I want my dog. I *need* my dog. I need him right now.' She was off her chair a second later, the panic on her face obvious to everyone in the room.

'I'll go with you,' Charles said calmly. 'I didn't know you had your dog with you or I would have insisted you bring him in with you.'

'If you know I wear flowered underwear and gargle with Listerine, how could you not know about my dog?' Kathryn snapped as she followed Charles out of the secret room.

'We know about your dog, Kathryn, we just didn't think you would bring him with you this evening. I apologize. Let me get you a slicker.'

'We don't have to go outside. All I have to do is whistle and click this remote,' she said pressing a small black box in her hand. 'The door to the cab will open and close on its

37

own. I didn't know about gadgets like this until after . . .
until after Alan died and I got my dog. He's been K-9
trained. Open the door. He'll find me.'

And he did. Charles stepped backward until his back
was pressed against the newel post on the stairway. In his
life he'd never seen a more magnificent dog. He said so
in a shaky voice.

'Charles, this is Murphy. I named him after the man
who taught me how to drive that rig out there. He was one
sorry son of a bitch. Shake hands, Murph.' The Belgian
Malinois held out his paw. Charles shook it manfully.
'Now, Murph, show him those beautiful teeth of yours.'
The dog obliged and growled as he did it, his lips pealing
back as his ears went flat against his head.

'How much does he weigh?' Charles asked nervously.

'One hundred and ten pounds,' Kathryn said smartly.
'I got him the day after Alan's funeral. I needed someone
in . . . in . . . in his seat. He was fully trained at the
time. He's three years old. He's been trained to kill if
necessary.'

Charles blinked at her flat, emotionless voice. 'Are you
ready to return to the others?'

'*We're* ready,' Kathryn said.

The panel in the wall moved quietly and closed just as
quietly.

'This is Murphy,' Kathryn said by way of introduction.
The collective gasp pleased her.

'I'm afraid of dogs,' Yoko said drawing her legs up
under her so they wouldn't dangle on the floor.

'Get over it because this dog goes where I go.' Her
voice was not unkind, just coolly matter-of-fact.

Yoko's feet stayed under her rump.

'*Sitz!*' The Malinois dropped to his haunches and then

stretched out at Kathryn's feet. 'He understands German as I do,' Kathryn explained.

'Tell us how you came to us and then tell us your story, Kathryn,' Myra said gently.

Kathryn ran her hands through her hair as she struggled for the words she needed and wanted to say. 'I've only ever talked about this once and that was to Nikki Quinn, the day after Alan's funeral. It wasn't easy then and it isn't easy now. I was walking down the street and there was this walk-in legal clinic where lawyers do pro bono work. I walked around the block a few times before I got up the courage to go inside. I waited seven years to tell my story and when I finally told it to Nikki Quinn she told me the statute of limitations had run out and there was nothing I could do legally.

'I'm very nervous talking about this. It's still as painful as the day it happened. It's like a beacon in the forefront of my mind. I've lived with it every hour of every day for seven long years.'

'You have to tell us everything, Kathryn. It's the only way we're going to be able to help you,' Myra said gently. 'Start at the beginning and tell us everything you can remember. We'll ask questions when you're finished. What kind of a day was it? Where were you headed? What were you hauling?'

Kathryn took a deep breath. 'It was a nice day. The sun was out. It was one of Alan's better days. He loved riding shotgun, as he called it. Listen, I need to tell you, right now, right up front, how much I loved that man. He was my white knight. He was the wind beneath my wings. He was the reason and the only reason I wanted to get up in the morning. He was my one true love. You need to know all this so you don't misjudge me or Alan when I finish my story.

'We were both orphans, both of us working our way through school. We met in one of our engineering classes. Back then we thought we were going to build a whole new world. In our third year, Alan was diagnosed with multiple sclerosis. He was one of the unfortunate ones because it attacked him quickly and viciously. By the time we graduated he was using a cane to get around. Suddenly building new worlds didn't seem important to either one of us. We both worked for a year and the money we saved during that year was used to put me through truck driving school. I made enough money the first couple of years to put a down payment on that rig out front.

'There were no remissions for Alan. He just got steadily worse. The day came when he couldn't walk anymore so I took on extra jobs to get the truck outfitted with a hydraulic lift so he could get in and out of the truck and then into a wheelchair. In addition to the multiple sclerosis, he was also diagnosed as having Parkinson's disease. He loved being on the road. It was what he lived for. He used to sing as we tooled along. He'd talk on the CB to other truckers. They all knew us. When we'd pull into a truck stop they'd always look after Alan so I could shower . He hated that part of it, but the other truckers were good to him. After a while it didn't matter. It was so hard for him in the beginning to let others see how incapacitated he was.

'We didn't have a house or a home base of any kind. We lived out of our truck. Sometimes, if there was a long layover, we'd camp out in a cheap motel. His medical bills bled me dry. He . . . loved me so much. Sometimes late at night I'd hear him cry. In the daytime, he kept this tight control. You know what I mean. I used to cry in the bathroom at the different truck stops and then wear my dark glasses so he wouldn't know. He always knew, though.

'That afternoon we drove into Bakersfield, California, to pick up a load of computers to be delivered up to Mojave and from there we were going on to Vegas with some repaired slot machines. We headed up Highway 58 through the Tehachapi Pass, delivered the computers to the military base and then stopped at the Starlite Cafe for fuel and to get something to eat. It wasn't one of my regular truck stops. I was starving so we stopped. I think I was there once before, but it was years and years ago. I was ahead of schedule by forty-five minutes that day.

'I got out of the truck, walked around to the passenger side and was getting Alan's wheelchair out of the special motorized compartment I had built behind the cab, when I heard . . .

. . . a loud roar that shook the ground. She swung around to admire the cycles. She and Alan had ridden during their first two years in college. In fact, they'd belonged to a motorcycle club. It had always been Alan's secret desire to own one of the 1930 Indians. She waved and smiled knowing Alan was probably admiring the Indians from his perch in the cab. Some of her fondest memories were of the little back road trips they used to take during those first two years of college.

'Hey, Red,' someone called out.

Kathryn whipped around, her hand going to her heart. 'You scared me there for a minute. How's it going?'

'Sorry. I didn't mean to frighten you. I was wondering if you needed any help.'

'Thanks but no. I do this all the time.'

41

Fern Michaels

'Is it for him?' the biker asked pointing to Alan who was staring at them through the window.

She stared up at Alan and smiled. He looked so anxious. 'I was admiring your motorcycles. Alan and I used to ride Indians. No other bike like them in the world.'

'You got that right, Red,' the biker said referring to Kathryn's mane of auburn curls.

'So what's wrong with him,' the biker asked bluntly.

'My husband has multiple sclerosis and Parkinson's disease.'

'Damn shame. Must be hard on you, Red.'

A chill washed up her spine. 'I manage,' she said curtly as she stepped away. She pulled the wheelchair closer. Out of the corner of her eye she saw two men in cycle garb step out from behind the back of the truck. Her heart took on extra beats as she tried to figure a way to outrun the men if need be. Why in the damn hell had she parked so far away from the main parking area? Because there had been no other spots available when she'd pulled in. Now the lot was practically deserted.

'I really have to get moving. Nice talking to you,' she said stepping closer to the cab door.

They came behind her, yanking her arms backward. The man she'd been talking to kicked the wheelchair away. She watched it skid across the parking lot. They ripped at her boots, at her clothes until she was naked and then they dragged her across the shallow ditch at the end of the parking area and into the undergrowth.

She tried to scream, but they chopped at her throat as she fought them with every ounce of strength in her body until she couldn't fight any longer. She closed her eyes and tried to put her mind and body in another place, a place that was warm and gentle, a place where Alan protected

42

her. She felt them change position, felt them roll her over, felt their hands, smelled their bodies. She knew she was crying, whimpering as they raped and sodomized her over and over again. If I ever find you, I'll kill you . . .

. . . but I never went after them.' She wiped at the tears streaming down her cheeks. 'I have all this evidence and it doesn't do me one little bit of good. All because of a stupid law. A damn stupid law that doesn't care about me or about Alan,' Kathryn said bitterly.

'Are you up to some questions, Kathryn?' Nikki asked.

'Sure. Nothing could be worse than saying all that out loud.'

'Why didn't your husband get on the CB or roll down the window and call for help? Why didn't he blow the horn? Why didn't you call for help?' Julia asked.

'I took the ignition key with me. The CB is powered. So are the windows and horn. I needed the key to open the compartment.'

'Maybe if he had opened his door . . .'

'No,' Kathryn interrupted. 'It wouldn't have helped. He couldn't get out and down without my help. I tried to call for help but they chopped my neck. I could only make croaking sounds. He did everything he could under the circumstances. He took their damn picture. We have a partial license plate. They were wearing jackets that said WEEKEND WARRIORS. That's a motorcycle club with a thousand different chapters all across the country. It's made up mostly of white-collar professionals.'

'Did you report the rape to the police?' Alexis asked.

Kathryn hung her head and mumbled, 'No. No, I didn't. The reason I didn't was Alan. He had a seizure and I had to think of him. I crawled back to the truck, found my clothes and the key that was in my shirt pocket. I was like a zombie, OK. I shifted into neutral and got dressed and went inside to get help for Alan. The paramedics came and revived him. I was *alive*. I wasn't sure about Alan. He was my primary concern. If you want to think that was stupid, go ahead and think it. There was no way in hell Alan could hold up to police questioning and a trial. Absolutely no way. Alan was never the same after that night. Neither was I, but I tried. Alan didn't seem to have a choice. He kept having more and more seizures. Then he had his last paralyzing stroke. He lost his will to live. I know that. I tried to keep him alive as long as I could. I did everything. Everything. If only you had known him when he was young. If only you had known the Alan I fell in love with. If you had known him, you would understand. I survived and he didn't. It's that simple.

'Here's my evidence,' Kathryn said tossing a packet on the table. 'You people sitting here make me remember why I didn't go to the police. They would have been just like you, questioning me, asking me questions like I was the one who did something wrong. I told you what happened. There's my proof. The partial license plate number. The picture Alan took. There's some definition to it. It needs to be enhanced. One of the bikers was named Lee. They belonged to the Weekend Warriors. I know what they looked like. I know how they smelled and I damn well know how they felt. Because of Alan, I waited too long. If I had to do it all over again, I wouldn't do anything different. If you people hadn't come along when you did, I would have started on my own search. Just because the eyes of the law are closed doesn't mean my eyes are closed. Alan's gone now. I don't care what happens to me.'

'You say that like you mean it,' Nikki said quietly.

'I do mean it,' Kathryn said coldly.

'And what would be your revenge against the men who did this to you, Kathryn?' Myra asked quietly.

Kathryn didn't blink or miss a beat. Head high, her shoulders back, the words shot out of her mouth like bullets. 'I want to slice off their goddamn balls with a dull knife.'

Three

The silence in the room was deafening. Kathryn raised her eyes and stared around at the group of women. 'You look shocked!' she said, wondering if it was what she'd said or the way she'd said it. 'I'm serious here. It's better than they deserve. You asked me a question and I gave you my answer. I didn't need to think about my answer because I've thought about nothing else for the past seven years.' Bitterness rang in her voice as she let her gaze sweep from one woman to the other, finally coming to rest on Charles who was staring at her intently, a look of compassion on his face.

'Obviously, none of you care for my answer. You know what, that's just too damn bad. I think I want to know a little more about how this is all going to work or I'm outta here with my dog. I don't have to prove anything to any of you. I came here because I thought you would help. You certainly led me to believe that was the case. I didn't come here to be judged.'

'Of course you've thought about it. You would have to be inhuman not to have thought about it. I'm sure we've all thought about how we want to be avenged. I know I have,' Myra said.

They all started to talk at once. Myra picked up her gavel and banged it three times on top of the polished table. 'One at a time, sisters. It's important for all of us to understand right now that each person's idea of vengeance and retribution is different from someone else's. I want each of you to tell me what you think would be a fitting punishment for the men who attacked and raped Kathryn. In the end, it has to be Kathryn's decision. Let's be clear on that. Isabelle, tell us what you think.'

Isabelle cleared her throat nervously as she fiddled with the long braid hanging down her back. 'I'm real big on an eye for an eye. I agree with Kathryn. I have to admit, I cheered that Bobbit woman.' She looked at Kathryn. 'I think your punishment is just.'

Yoko clapped her hands against her cheeks. 'What about their families? What if they have wives? Maybe the wives don't know their husbands . . . do . . . things like that. It will be like you are punishing them for something they did not do.'

Nikki responded, 'Obviously they weren't thinking of their wives when they attacked Kathryn. We have to stay focused and remember that our issue is with the criminals not their families.'

'Alexis, what's your opinion?' Myra asked.

'You play you pay. Kathryn is right. They didn't think about their families or their wives. They were out for a good time and the hell with everything else. They goddamn violated her and they should be made to pay for what they did. I agree with Kathryn. Let's slice their balls off and pickle them. We can send them their balls anonymously. Yeah, yeah, I like that,' Alexis said vehemently.

Charles straightened his tie as his gaze swept across the ceiling. A smile tugged at the corners of his mouth and did not go unnoticed by Kathryn.

'Julia, what do you think?' Myra asked.

Kathryn jerked upright at the doctor's cold, deadly voice. 'I'll do the operation. I'll use my dullest surgical knife. I will place all testicles in formaldehyde and will label each jar. I will even mail them. Does that answer your question?'

'Yes,' Myra said. 'Yoko?'

Yoko looked first at one woman and then another as she struggled to find the words she wanted. She stared at the shoebox in the middle of the table.

Kathryn leaned over and pinched Murphy's ear. The huge dog reared back and stood up. 'What's your damn problem, Yoko?' Kathryn said as her foot pressed against the dog's foot to make him turn around until he was facing Yoko. 'You should be chomping at the bit to go after these guys. Wasn't your father just like them? Your history says he was.'

'Well . . . I . . .' Yoko's eyes filled with tears.

Kathryn jabbed her finger in Yoko's direction. 'You better not turn out to be a weak link, sister. I'm not putting my ass on the line, and I don't think these other women will either, if you have to sit and ponder everything and then weasel out when the going gets tough. I think you're too wishy-washy for my taste. I'm going to keep my eye on you. This dog is going to do the same thing. Now, what the hell is your answer?'

'I apologize if I don't think fast enough for you, Kathryn. I feel you are justified in wanting revenge. What you propose is drastic. You said yourself you are alive and well. Perhaps not mentally well but well just the same. I am most sorry about your husband's death. Your grief is palpable. I understand this. I will vote no this time because I do not know these men.'

49

'You know, Yoko, by coming here tonight you pledged to be her sister. It's not important for you to know the men,' Julia hissed between her teeth. 'You had better not turn into a weak link because if you do, I'll go after you myself.'

Myra nodded. 'Your decision is recorded, Yoko. Nikki?'

Nikki thought about all the rape cases she'd taken to court and lost. Cases where the rape victim was raped twice, once by a man and then again by the courts. 'I agree,' she said, her voice ringing out loud and clear.

'I vote yes also,' Myra said.

'Your revenge is approved by the majority of the sisters, Kathryn.'

'Now we need to set up an airtight, working plan. I think this is the time when we need Charles's input. Charles worked for the British government at MI6 and he was an excellent operative until his cover was blown. The government then made sure he was led to safety here in the United States. We can trust him and we can rely on him.'

Charles stood up, every inch the stiff upper lipped Brit. 'What we have here,' he said waving his arm about, 'is a multimillion dollar command center. There is absolutely nothing we can't find out about anybody. I know many people who will help us just for the joy of helping to right old wrongs. There are no codes that can't be broken. I was taught to do this early on in my career and I've stayed up on the latest developments. I'm only telling you this in case we come up against some coded messages or the like. I believe I know just about everything there is to know about encryption. These sophisticated computers and their memory banks rival those at the CIA. I personally built them. Any questions so far?'

The women all shook their heads.

'Good. Then I'll continue. This is how I see it. Obviously the men who attacked Kathryn live somewhere in the state of California. I feel confidant in saying somewhere within a five hundred-mile radius of where Kathryn was attacked. I see this as a four man, excuse me, woman job.' Charles's gaze raked the room as he tried to decide which three women would work best with Kathryn in the lead.

Isabelle tugged at her braid, her hands shaking. 'I have a question. Maybe it's more of a statement. If this means going to California, I'm afraid I can't go. If I don't work, I won't be able to pay my rent. I can't afford to take any time off. If there's something I can do from this end, I'll be more than happy to comply.'

'Isabelle, your bank account is quite robust these days. Your next statement will reflect a transfer of money. You have nothing to worry about, dear. We also paid up your rent and your health insurance a year in advance. Your time is now your sisters' time. This was just a little down payment in advance until we can right your cause,' Myra said. Isabelle nodded gratefully.

'Is anyone else worried about time away?' Charles asked.

'I do not think I can leave the nursery and my husband. He would not understand,' Yoko said.

Kathryn stood up, her arms flying upward. Murphy reared up, his ears going flat against his head. 'That's it! That's it! Just tell me what the hell you're doing here? Did you think this was going to be some kind of tea party? Don't give me any of that Asian different culture crap either. For starters, I don't want you on my case. All I have to do is look at you to know you're about as dependable as shit.'

The picture of serenity, Yoko replied,'You are a hot-head, Kathryn.'

Taken aback, Kathryn responded bluntly, the way she did to everything, 'That's true, I am. I'm also kind, considerate, thoughtful and I'm damn loyal to those near and dear to me. When I give my word I keep it. What's your *shtick*?'

'I am all those things myself, Kathryn. I did not know what to expect when I came here this evening. Now that I know what is expected, I will make arrangements so that I can fulfill my duties to this organization. I wish only to be helpful to all of you. If you have difficulty with my ways, you must tell me. I have no wish to be like you. I want only to be able to understand and act within my own boundaries. You need have no fear of me being, what you called, the weak link. I am very strong, mentally and physically. I had to be, to survive. I just want to help so that when it is my turn you will want to help me.'

Kathryn grimaced. 'OK, OK, but I'm still going to keep my eye on you.'

'And mine will be on you, also, Kathryn.'

'What's next?' Nikki asked, looking at Myra.

The room grew still. Even Charles looked up from the computer he was working on.

'I think we should go into the house and have some food while Charles works on the computers. It is late and we have all day tomorrow to finalize our plans. Is that agreeable to everyone?'

'I must go home,' Yoko said.

'No. You will stay,' Myra said coolly. 'Nikki explained all this to you in advance. Please don't bring this to a test,

Yoko. If you do, you will not like the outcome. My arms are long and they stretch quite far.'

Yoko bowed. 'I will stay then. I wish to see in writing the next time what the rules are for me.'

'The same rules apply to each of us. You aren't special so don't pretend to be something you aren't. You speak fluent English and you graduated college. You were born in this country so don't give us that Asian stuff. I read your dossier,' Kathryn snapped irritably.

'We'll see you in the morning, Charles. Would you like some coffee or a sandwich?'

'There can't be food or drink in here, Myra. I'll get something later. We'll meet in the dining room at eight tomorrow morning if that's all right with everyone. Good night, ladies.'

Everyone except Nikki passed on the offer of food and headed for the staircase that would take them to the second floor. Kathryn walked to the door and let Murphy out. She waited until he returned and then slammed and locked the heavy door.

The storm continued to rage as Nikki followed Myra into the kitchen. 'I'm starved. Did Charles make anything good for us?'

'There's a ham and a breast of turkey. Would you like me to make some coffee?'

'Myra, what I would really like is a good triple shot of your best scotch. I think I'll have a ham and turkey sandwich. That's a no on the coffee.'

Myra measured coffee into the stainless steel basket. At Nikki's questioning look, she said, 'It's for me. Charles will be in later and I know he'll want coffee. How do you think it went, Nikki?'

'I'm not sure, Myra. It got a little tense there for a

minute. For the first shot out of the gate, I guess it went OK. This was our first meeting. No one really knew what to expect. I think things will fall into place in the morning when Charles shows us what he's retrieved from all those computers. Once we set up a plan, things will level off. The women have to get to know one another. It's the unknown that is throwing everyone into a flap. As much as I hate to admit it, I think it's all going to work out.' She leaned her elbows on the table and stared at the sugar bowl.

Myra nodded. She knew this beautiful girl sitting across from her as well as she knew herself. 'There's something bothering you, Nikki. Do you want to talk about it or is it something personal between you and Jack?'

'I do need to talk, Myra. One of my paralegals told me she saw Jack having dinner with a beautiful redhead the other night. It bothers me. I'm feeling kind of betrayed right now. Marie Lewellen's case goes to court next month. I've used up my last postponement. I can't win it, Myra. Jack knows I'm just going through the motions. He's taking the whole thing personally. I hate it when he does that. You should have heard him the day you posted Marie's bail. He was like a rooster in a duck pond. Did you . . . ah . . . decide when you're going to spirit her and her family away?'

'It's better if you don't know, Nikki. Just go about your daily business the same way you always do.'

'Myra, that's goddamn near impossible. I don't have a normal life anymore. I'm up to my eyeballs in illegalities, I could lose my license to practice law, I've lost my boyfriend who was supposed to put a ring on my finger this year, and I damn near cheered when those women voted to castrate those creeps that attacked Kathryn. What does that make me, Myra? Tell me. I need to know what I'm turning into here.'

'Jack will come back, dear. I'm sure the dinner with the redhead was a witness or a friend. Jack loves you. If you lose your license, we'll have Charles get you a new identity. You know, Nikki, it really isn't all that hard to do if you have the right contacts. You aren't turning into anything. You are still the bright, intelligent girl I love and admire. *You* haven't changed. Circumstances have changed.'

Nikki bit into her sandwich. She chewed thoughtfully. 'I can't be on Kathryn's team this time around. I have to be here for Marie. After that, I'm all yours. I will take some of that coffee, Myra. By the way, that was a nice thing you did for Isabelle. She's been having a terrible time.'

'We'll get her life back for her. If she's the kind of person I think she is, she'll pay me back as soon as possible. I like Kathryn. I wanted to cry for her. I like all the women. It's all so unjust, so unfair. But then that's why we formed the Sisterhood, isn't it?' Myra said reassuringly, then added, 'Nikki, how will you handle it when Marie Lewellen . . . disappears?'

'Very carefully, Myra. Have you been in touch with her lately?'

'Goodness, no. I've stayed away just the way you said I should. She sent me a note thanking me for posting her bail. I haven't called either. Have you seen her?'

Nikki pushed her plate to the center of the table. 'No. I do talk to her on the phone. She told me her husband took his vacation. She said he had something like forty-five days coming to him and was going to do some things to the house. Their pictures are going to be all over the news and in the newspapers. Where are you going to relocate them?'

'It's better if you don't know, Nikki. Julia Webster is going to do some plastic surgery on both Marie and her husband once they're settled in their new home. Children change on a day-to-day basis. We'll have them home schooled for a year or so until we feel they've changed enough not to warrant scrutiny. We have it under control, dear.'

'OK, I'm off to bed.' She looked around. 'I always loved this kitchen. I mean, I really loved it.'

Myra nodded. 'I'll clean up here and make some sandwiches for Charles for later. I know, Nikki, that you still have mixed feelings about what we're doing. I'm hoping in time you will grow as comfortable with it as I have. If not, you'll just have to suck it up,' Myra said cheerfully.

In spite of herself, Nikki burst out laughing. She hugged Myra good night before she headed up the kitchen staircase that would take her to her old room at the end of the long hall that ran the length of the house.

'Screw you, Jack,' she muttered as she pulled off her sweat pants. As she tugged at the bottom of the pant legs she saw the dark red X on the hem. Barbara always made a red X on her jeans and sweats so they wouldn't mix them up in the laundry. Tears burned her eyes and trickled down her cheeks as her index finger traced the X. 'We're doing it for you, Barb. Wherever you are, I hope you understand. I miss you, Barb. I'd give anything if I could talk to you about Jack. Watch over us, OK?' She didn't feel the least bit silly or self-conscious talking to someone who wasn't there. Barbara's spirit would always live in this room. The faint scent of her perfume still lingered in the air after all this time. She knew in her heart it would stay in the room forever, just like the furniture would stay as well as her clothes and her skis. She looked over at the rocker that was moving slowly back and forth.

Nikki walked over to the old rocker and placed her hand on the arm rest to stop the chair from moving. It continued to rock.

'What's your problem, Nik?'

Nikki yelped and ran back to the bed. 'Barb?'

'Yes.'

'Is it really you?'

'In spirit. Do you want to give me a quiz?'

Nikki shook her head. Was she dreaming? 'I'm glad you're here. At least I think I'm glad you're here. I need to talk to you about Jack. I need to talk to you about a lot of things. You know what's going on, don't you?'

'Every single thing. I have one kick-ass mother, don't I? If you're asking me if I approve, I do. Get them all, Nik. Make them pay for what they did to those women. I hope you can continue to do it forever. It's about time someone took matters into their own hands. I wish I was there to help you. Just promise me you won't get caught.'

Nikki laughed. 'I'll do my best not to get caught. Can you just picture me in the slammer?'

'No, I can't picture that at all. Promise me you'll be careful. I wish I was there to help you and Mom and all those women.'

'God, I wish that so much, Barb. I miss you. It's always worse here in this room. It's like you're still here. I can smell your perfume. I can see your skis leaning up in the corner and your mom gave me your sweat pants tonight. I started to cry when I saw the red X on the bottom of the pants leg. Jack had dinner with some good-looking redhead. My paralegal saw them.

'They look good on you. Let's get back to Jack. He's

*just trying to tick you off, Nik. Guys do that as you and
I both found out along the way. He knew your paralegal
would tell you she saw him with some good-looking chick.
You aren't going to fall for that, are you, Nik?'*

'It doesn't matter. It still hurts. So, how . . . how is it
on the . . . other side?'

*'Peaceful. Quiet. Beautiful. We were talking about
Jack . . .'*

'He's so competitive. I can't win the case with Marie
Lewellen. We all knew that going in. You know the drill,
open mouth, insert foot. He took me on. My name is going
to be mud when Marie disappears. I'm not calling him so
don't even suggest it.'

*'I wasn't going to suggest any such thing. Why don't
you call up Mike Deverone and ask him out to dinner. He
always had the hots for you. And he has a brain plus he's
an excellent lawyer, as you well know.'*

'That's a thought.'

*'How come I always have to do your thinking for
you. Where's 'Willie? Toss him over here, OK. I miss
the little guy.'*

Nikki walked over to the twin bed Barbara had always
slept in. She pulled down the spread and raised the pillow.
She hugged the little bear before she tossed it in the
direction of the rocking chair. She almost fainted when
she saw the little bear swirl in mid air and then stop as
though someone had reached for it. She plopped down
on the edge of her own bed, her emotions running wild
as she stared across the room at the rocking chair.

'Listen, are you going to . . . you know, hang around
or do you have to . . . go . . . back. I'm dead on my . . .
sorry, I'm out on my feet and I have to get up early.'

'I thought I would sit here and rock with Willie for a

while. You don't mind, do you? I'll watch over you while you sleep, Nik.'
'No, I don't mind. Barb, do you come here . . . often? If I need you, what should I do?'
'Just call my name. Hey, isn't there a song by that name?'
'Probably. There's a song for everything just like there's a book for everything in the world. There's even a song for pantyhose. You should hear that one. Someone with red hair named Corinda Carford sings it. You'd get a kick out of it, Barb, because you always hated pantyhose. I have the CD in my apartment if you ever want to hear it.'
'OK. Good night, Nik. Sweet dreams. Don't forget to blow out the candle.'
'Night, Barb.' Nikki cupped her hands around the flame and blew it out as instructed.
'Good girl. Now, go to sleep.'
Nikki crunched her pillow into a ball under her head. One eye open, one eye closed, she listened as the rocker moved back and forth on the pine floors, the sound finally lulling her into a deep, dreamless sleep.

Four

Murphy nosed open the swinging door that led to the dining room where a buffet was set up on the sideboard. Charles, wearing a pristine white chef's coat, presided over the wide array of food. Myra was already seated at the head of the table, her napkin spread on her lap. She looked regal as always. She motioned for the women to take their seats.

'Good morning, ladies. I trust you slept well,' Charles said.

The women nodded as he poured orange juice from a crystal pitcher into elegant goblets. Myra poured the coffee from an antique, silver pot that had once belonged to her great grandmother.

'For breakfast we have ham, bacon, sausage, kippers, scones, eggs Benedict, waffles, pancakes and a banana pear compote. Tell me what you would like and it will be my pleasure to serve you,' Charles said.

Kathryn giggled. 'I'll have one of everything and Murphy gets the same. He eats what I eat. Who cooked all this? No offense, Myra, but you don't look like the type who cooks.'

Myra smiled. 'I told you Charles was a man of many talents. He prepared breakfast. He graciously allowed me to do the place setting. I apologize for the lack of flowers on the table.'

'Are the telephones working yet?' Yoko queried.

'Unfortunately, no.' Yoko dropped her gaze to stare at her lap.

Kathryn bristled as the others all started to talk at once.

'Is the power on?' Julia asked.

'Yes, the power came on around six this morning just as Charles was finishing up his work. I really don't like to talk about business at meal time so let's speak of pleasantries,' Myra said as she buttered a scone, Charles's specialty.

'Tell us about this old house,' Alexis said. 'It's beautiful. I just love old houses that are steeped in charm and character. I bought a little house before . . . you know, *before*. It was a cozy little bungalow with a garden bathroom and a real fireplace. I had window boxes jampacked with flowers and I had these clay pots of flowers on each side of the steps. I just loved that little house.'

'Past tense, Alexis?' Isabelle said.

'I had to sell it to help pay my legal fees. I have a small apartment now with a shower and no bathtub.'

'That's all going to change, dear. I promise,' Myra said. 'You asked about this house. It's over three hundred years old. It spreads out over three hundred acres. My neighbors are a mile away in each direction. We really are secluded which works to our advantage. My family was always interested in upholding the rights of others and preserving justice. My great grandfather was a judge and so was my grandfather. My parents and grandparents never *owned* slaves. They had paid workers and after so many years of service, each family was given a generous plot of land.

Pinewood originally consisted of over a thousand acres. All but the remaining three hundred acres that I own were given away to the people who worked for our family. My grandparents, along with several other families, aided the runaway slaves through the tunnels under the house.

'I feel like I'm now in a position to do my part by carrying out my ancestors' tradition of helping others,' she concluded.

'This looks absolutely delicious,' Nikki said digging into her eggs Benedict.

'If there's nothing else I can serve you ladies, I'll leave you and meet up with you again in our command center, in, let's say, ninety minutes. Enjoy your breakfast.'

'Wherever did you find that jewel of a man?' Julia asked.

'I knew Charles in my youth. My parents at the time didn't think his lifestyle was befitting a southern lady like myself, so after three months in Europe they dragged me back home,' Myra drawled. 'I married and took over the candy company. It was just a short time later when our offices got a call from the British government asking if Charles could be relocated here to us in the United States because Charles's life was in danger. We said yes and he took over the security of the firm. It was the best decision I ever made. We both retired at the same time. And now, we've all arrived at this place in time. With Charles's expertise, we're going to make the Sisterhood work for all of us.'

Nikki stood up and patted her stomach. 'That was a wonderful breakfast and I ate way too much. Would anyone like more coffee?' she asked.

'Fill it up,' Kathryn said holding up her cup.

'I've had my limit,' Isabelle said.

Alexis and Julia shook their heads.

'I would prefer tea,' Yoko said.

Kathryn rolled her eyes. 'Now, why did I know you were going to say that. When in Rome . . .'

Myra stood up in the hopes of warding off another verbal confrontation between Yoko and Kathryn. 'I'd like you to meet my ancestors,' she said, pointing to the various old fashioned sepia toned pictures in heavy gilt frames. 'This is my mother and father. On the far wall are my grandparents and next to them, their parents. The other family members, and there are many, are on the wall going up the staircase. This is my daughter Barbara when she was six. It was her first pony,' Myra said pointing to a modern painting over the sideboard. 'You might not recognize her, but the picture next to Barbara, on her first pony, is our Nikki. They were both such sturdy little girls,' she said with a catch in her voice.

'Our ninety minutes are about up, Myra. We both know Charles doesn't like to be kept waiting. I can clear things up here and join you when I'm finished, if that's all right with you,' Nikki said in an effort to drive away the stricken look on Myra's face.

'Of course, dear. We can fill you in when you join us,' Myra said leading the parade out of the dining room and down the hall to the living room. Within minutes they were all seated at the round table, their faces expectant as Charles waved a sheaf of papers.

Charles walked around the table much the way a teacher does when giving a test.

'The computers are still working and these things take time but this is what I was able to retrieve. There are motorcycle groups and organizations in every one of our fifty states. There are as many as ninety such organizations in some states while others may only have three or four. I have here eight thousand clubs. I was able to whittle that number down to forty-seven when I asked the computer to flush out just Indian motorbikes. In addition to the forty-seven organizations, there are splinter groups that I was able to track down. Sometimes they spring up overnight so the count is not as accurate as I would like. I further condensed the number when I asked for just Weekend Warriors. The computer tells me there are twenty-nine Weekend Warrior groups. From those twenty-nine groups, nine cells have splintered off and are now calling themselves Road Warriors. A total of eleven groups that meet our criteria are located in California.

'I filled out an application to join both the Weekend Warriors as well as the Road Warriors. My applications arrived while we were having breakfast. I faxed it back moments ago. When you're accepted, you're given a handbook with the rules and regulations, dates and times of meetings, proposed road trips, a calendar of events, as well as a list of all the members along with their addresses and phone numbers. This only happens after you pay your dues, which is quite hefty at nine hundred dollars a year. You have to send them a scanned picture of yourself which I did. I gave them my credit card number as well. As soon as it clears, I have the choice of having them overnight the materials, or I will be given a password and I can download said material. I'm electing to download. The faxes should be coming through any minute now and Kathryn can see if her attackers still belong to either group.'

'Way to go, Charlessss,' Kathryn chortled. He preened for her benefit. The others clapped their hands in glee.

'What'd I miss, what'd I miss?' Nikki said taking

her seat at the table. 'By the way, the power went out again.'

Myra shrugged. 'We'll fill you in later, dear. Just listen to Charles for now. He is absolutely amazing.'

'I then checked the Department of Motor Vehicles and managed to secure the license plates for the Indian motorcycles in those nine groups.' Charles took a deep breath and stared straight at Kathryn. 'I found one plate with the same three numbers you gave us. I now have the full license plate number. It belongs to Dr Clark Wagstaff. He's an oral surgeon in Los Angeles. I ran a D and B on him and the report just came back. Dr Wagstaff owns the medical building he practices in. His net worth, excluding the medical building, is around nine million. He takes in over a million dollars a year after taxes. I'm checking his income tax records. That might take a little longer but I will have answers for you by the end of the day. Possibly sooner.'

Kathryn's clenched fists shot upward. 'Yessss. What about the one they called Lee? Were you able to pull up anything on him?'

'I won't know about Lee until the rest of the faxes come through. I tend to think he's a colleague or possibly a business partner. I think it's safe to say the third man is either a relative or another colleague.'

The phone on the fax machine rang. Charles smiled. The women sat back, their eyes glued to the machine next to Charles.

Twenty minutes later Charles stacked the faxed sheets into the printer and made copies for each woman. He handed them out. 'My job for the moment is done. What you have to do now is come up with a plan to bring these three men together. I'm going to see if I can catch an hour or so of sleep. Which one of you really knows your way around a computer? Nikki?'

'I'm pretty good at it. Why?'

'Let me show you. When Kathryn identifies the three men, I want you to log on to this particular computer and type in the name. Send it as an email to this address,' he said pointing to an email address on a yellow pad next to the computer bank. 'In an hour's time you will have a report on each man from the day they were born. Can you handle it, Nikki?'

'Yes. Charles, who does this email address belong to?' Nikki hissed as a vision of the FBI, the CIA and Washington, DC's District Attorney, Jack Emery, all pounding on Myra's front door, flashed in front of her eyes.

'Why, the Queen, of course. Ask a silly question and you get a silly answer. I'll see you all in a bit.'

Myra picked up her pen and yellow pad. 'You need a plan, Kathryn. Something that will entice these men to want to participate. You said you and your husband used to ride. What was it you liked? What kind of invitation would you consider accepting? Just how enthusiastic are bikers.'

Kathryn talked as she flipped through the faxes. 'Bikers are a breed unto themselves. Alan and I weren't bikers in the true sense of the word. We used to do back road trails just for fun on weekends. It's the speed, the wind in your face, your hair flying behind you. That part isn't the same anymore because the laws have changed and now you have to wear helmets. It's that free spirit thing everyone aspires to. Then there's the camaraderie, the stories. You know, like fishermen when they say they caught a *really* big one. Maybe a contest. All expenses paid. Perhaps a prize that would be impossible to turn down. The prize could be a mint condition Indian if you could manage to get your hands on one. I have to tell you they are almost impossible to find. A mint condition Indian would definitely raise the stakes.'

Myra scribbled on her pad. 'I think Charles will be able to find us one.'

'No, Myra, you don't understand. We don't need an actual bike. We're just going to say that on the invitation to whet their appetite, to make them want to do whatever it is we come up with. We're only inviting the three of them, right?' Kathryn asked. She flipped more pages and finally let out a whoop. 'This one!' she said waving the paper high in the air. 'Lee Sidney!'

'Two down and one to go. Keep looking, Kathryn,' Nikki said.

Isabelle interrupted. 'No, no, no. You have to invite a select group and you really do need to have the bike as a prize. Invite maybe a dozen or so besides the three in question. It will make it look more real. You will have to award the bike to one of the others to avoid questions later on. When the trip is over, we spirit the three away and no one will be the wiser.'

'This is not going to be the piece of cake you think it is. If these men have wives, we have to set something up for them so they don't go yapping to the cops. Maybe we could tell them they all won a trip to the Golden Door or something. Or a package deal, the wives get the spa and the guys get the road trip. Then you have to allow for the time we snatch them. How many days? And what about their offices? Are they going to be closed, open, what?' Alexis said as she doodled on the pad in front of her. 'We have to get them back here so Julia can slice and dice.

Then we have to get them back to California. It could get hairy.'

'We can use my rig for transport. Cycles and all. Five days driving cross country. Five days back. Maybe four if we push it. That's eight or nine days just driving time. And that's not allowing for sleep. We need time for Julia to hack off their balls. Unless she does it in back of the truck. We can spray some Lysol or something. What kind of time are we looking at, Julia?' Kathryn stopped turning the pages of the faxes. 'This is the third one,' she said, her voice filled with venom. 'Samuel La Fond.' She handed the sheet to Nikki.

'Sixteen hours at least. They'll be sedated. I don't have a problem doing it in back of the truck,' Julia said.

'OK. We'll drop them off at some place close to the area where the ride is to take place. I think it's definitely a plan. What do you think, Yoko?' Kathryn asked.

'I think it will work. I would like to offer a suggestion. After . . . after the surgery you will want to stay to see their reaction. That will not be a good thing, Kathryn. I think you should go to their offices first so you can look at them in the bright light. You have waited many years for this. Do not deprive yourself of seeing them in their own environment. It is unlikely they will recognize you. Although, you might have to dye your hair or Alexis can change your appearance someway. I think it will help you to see them before . . . before they have their respective surgeries. That is all I have to say.'

'Yoko, I think you're absolutely right. What do the rest of you think? Is it a good idea or not?' Kathryn asked.

'Very good,' Nikki said. 'Yoko is right, once you dump them you have to get far away. It's a rough plan but doable. Now we need to give some thought

69

to what they'll do when they pull their pants down for the first time. Are they going to go to the police? Will they call the other guys who were on the trip to find out if they're minus any of their body parts? They're going to be together so that means they're going to discover their . . . respective surgeries around the same time. If you were the only one they attacked, Kathryn, they're going to put two and two together. If attacking women is a pastime with them, they won't know who to blame. The police will have to ask a lot of questions. They aren't going to admit they raped anyone. We need to think about this a minute. What would be the charge if they reported it? In all the years of practicing law, this . . . this type of . . . case never came up.'

'Grand theft of the genitalia,' Alexis volunteered. She did her best not to laugh out loud.

'Police reports are a matter of public record. They could print the report in the newspaper. How's that going to look? They'll have to leave the country.' Isabelle smirked.

'They won't tell their friends because part of the biker psyche is that testosterone thing. They'll be like wild animals till they figure it out. They could come after you, Kathryn. Bikers are like truckers. They take care of their own. I saw that on a documentary once,' Myra said. 'What do you think, Nikki?'

'I think you're right. I think you were their one shot, Kathryn. The time was right for them. The situation felt right, where you parked, your incapacitated husband, the whole thing. If they're pillars of their community – and they probably are – they wouldn't risk doing something that terrible again and again. What you're going to need, Kathryn, is an airtight alibi for the time in question.

70

Isabelle is about your height and Alexis can make her look enough like you to pass muster. We can have her go to a resort or something, register under your name, use your credit card. She'll make herself scarce so people don't get a good look at her. A good red wig, a little patching here and there with some spirit gum and voila, she's you. Can you deal with that, Kathryn?'

'Absolutely.'

Almost to the minute of Charles' prediction, the email pinged to announce an incoming email. 'Oh, excuse me, incoming mail,' Nikki said getting up from the table.

Nikki pressed download and waited for the sent material to complete the transition. She then clicked the print icon and waited. Page after page shot out of the printer with amazing speed. She scooped up the pages before she transferred them to the copy machine and printed out nine copies. One copy for everyone plus one extra. She was about to hit the delete button a second later when the email disappeared in front of her eyes. She felt a chill wash up her spine. She added the extra set of papers to the bottom of her own report.

'My goodness,' Myra said. 'This is so thorough. I suggest we read them in silence and then discuss each man. Do you all approve?' The women nodded as they lowered their heads to read the reports in front of them.

A long time later, Myra removed her glasses and looked around at the women. 'This is the most amazing thing I've ever read. These men are such upstanding citizens it boggles my mind: they sit on various charitable boards; they donate handsomely to many worthy causes; all three are incredibly wealthy; their children go to Ivy League colleges; their wives do volunteer work; they all donate one day a week at a free clinic; they go to church on

Sunday with their wives; they play golf one day a month. Two weekends a month they take road trips with the Weekend Warriors. They've never been caught in an uncompromising position and there is no hint of scandal attached to them in any way. The three of them have been friends since college days and they're well thought of with their patients and have a thriving, lucrative practice. They do not falsify insurance records and they don't cheat on their income taxes.

'Each of them has an Indian and something called a Harley Hog. That about sums it up, sisters.'

'That's a pretty impressive report,' Kathryn said quietly. She looked at the faces staring at her. 'I'm not saying they aren't all those things. They raped me and the one named Lee sodomized me. That should be added to the report.' Her voice turned desperate sounding when she added, 'They stripped me naked and knew my husband was watching when they did all those things to me. That makes them no better than wild animals in my eyes.'

'I think your gums just started to recede, Kathryn. I'll call and make an appointment for you. In the meantime, we have the rest of the day to fine tune our plan. Choose your partners for this project and tell me when you feel you'll be ready to leave. You have a month to complete this project. You must be back here by the first Monday of the month at which time we'll pick our second case.'

'I need to take Murphy outside. He needs some exercise. Is it OK?' Kathryn asked.

'Of course. Come along, dear. I think we could all use a break about now. I can make some coffee and some tea for Yoko. The phone lines might be repaired and hopefully, the power is on. Charles said he was going to gas up the kitchen generator, so let's hope he did or we'll be drinking soda pop.'

Kathryn headed for the front door, Isabelle and Alexis headed for the stairs and the upstairs bathroom, while Myra, Nikki, Yoko and Julia walked toward the kitchen. Outside in the bright sunshine, Kathryn walked alongside her dog. She raised her eyes once to look upward. She muttered under her breath, words she'd said thousands of times, always under her breath. Except that one time when Alan had his last seizure and she'd screamed at the top of her lungs because she couldn't take it one day longer. Her husband had just stared at her and then closed his eyes. She knew in that one split second that he'd finally given up. Two hours later she held him in her arms and kissed him for the last time.

'I hope you can hear me, Alan. It's payback time!'

Murphy nudged her leg.

'I'm OK, Murphy. I'm OK now.'

Five

The TV wall monitor blossomed into life with a *zzzzzing* sound. The figure of the Scales of Justice consumed the entire screen within seconds. Kathryn felt like she should stand up and voice a loud cheer. She thought about it a second longer and then she did it, a look of pure joy on her face. 'Hey, she's my kind of lady! I'm taking that blindfold to mean she's looking the other way because the other way sucks. OK, that's it, that's all I have to say.' Her voice was sheepish sounding. The others smiled.

Charles hit the computer keys, the clicking sound loud in the quiet room. A map of the state of California appeared. He clicked again and again, localizing different areas, talking and explaining as map after map took over the screen. 'You need to decide on a specific area for your proposed road trip. Once you've settled on a route, we can fine tune it so we don't have any glitches. I took the liberty of making a list of twelve possible candidates for the trip. I selected four Road Warriors and eight Weekend Warriors plus the three "special guests." We'll have a total of fifteen cycles on the trip. Since our three nefarious cyclists live in the Los Angeles area, it would seem logical to start the trip there.

'I would like to make a suggestion here. Lone Pine is

about six hours from Los Angeles and about four hours north from where you were attacked, Kathryn. It's remote but there is a little town. The overnight camp stay, if that's what you're considering, could take place in the Alabama Hills. If you're planning on taking your truck, Kathryn, it would have to be parked on a dedicated road so as not to leave tire marks.' He clicked the keys and a map of Lone Pine appeared. 'I'll print these out for you and an alternative route if you decide this doesn't fit your needs.'

'How are we going to decide who wins the Indian?' Kathryn asked.

Myra smiled and reached to the middle of the table for the shoebox. 'The same way we chose your case to be first. It's called the luck of the draw. Very apropos, don't you think?'

'I like it,' Yoko smiled. The others beamed their approval.

'Then what?' Julia asked.

'Then they make camp, build a fire, have a few drinks followed by dinner at the restaurant in town. Assuming there is a restaurant in Lone Pine. Where, as luck would have it, we are sitting there in our biker duds, you know, tight black leather pants, our tits half hanging out of our vests, lots of silver stud jewelry, our Harleys parked out front, courtesy of my truck and Myra. The wealthy philanthropist, Charles, in disguise, will appear with the shoebox and a certificate of ownership for the Indian that will be shipped to the lucky person in a fortnight. How's that, Charles. A fortnight is two weeks, right?'

Charles allowed himself a small smile. 'Correct.'

'We party hearty, make sure the others get back to camp while one of us keeps our three busy. We then load them

76

and their bikes into my truck and split. When the others wake in the morning, they'll have mega hangovers and just assume our three got lucky with us three and head off home. I think it will work once, as Charles puts it, he's fine-tuned the whole scenario. What do you all think? Will it fly?'

The women's heads bobbed up and down.

'OK, this is what we need in the way of material things. Sisters, get your pencils ready. We need three Harley Hogs. That's so they'll take us seriously. Women on Hogs are special. Trust me on that. They'll be brand new, Myra, so you can resell them to get your money back afterward.' Myra waved her hand in dismissal to show she wasn't concerned about the cost.

'We have my truck. Julia knows what we'll need for her list and will write everything down or bring it from her office. Whatever works for her. Alexis will need to replenish her disguise trunk or whatever she uses to change our appearances. We'll need biker duds, the leather – second hand would be best so they look worn in – and push-up bras as our tits have to be up and almost out of the vests. Lots of silver junk stud jewelry. Worn boots in our size so we don't get blisters.'

'Why do our tits have to hang out?' Yoko asked, her face miserable. 'My breasts are small.'

'Because they do,' Julia said. 'Alexis can build you up with that putty stuff. You can be a 36 B if you want. You might be a little top heavy but you won't be bending over so it shouldn't be a problem.'

Yoko's almond shaped eyes literally turned round. 'You can do this?' she said directing her question to Alexis.

'Honey, I can give you a set of knockers that will blow any man's socks off,' Alexis grinned.

Myra laughed aloud while Charles turned about, his ears and neck bright red.

'I accept,' Yoko said smartly.

'Done,' Kathryn said smacking the table top. 'What's next?'

'What's next are the wives,' Nikki said. 'I think it should be a separate entity and not part of the bike deal. We'll send them two weeks ahead of the bike trip and then they have two weeks afterward. That will also make it easier for the men to accept the road trip without harping wives. Their kids are all in college so that won't pose any problems. Myra, you will be the wealthy female philanthropic person who donates these three free months to their wives. All three of them do volunteer charity work according to the dossier Charles printed out. Just pick out an organization they help out, make it your pet charity and award the certificates. How does that sound?'

'I love it,' Myra said. 'Thank you for giving me a job to do. I was afraid I would have to sit here and wait for details.' She looked so pleased, so grateful, Nikki found herself smiling.

'You are the CIC, Myra. You need to keep your hand in all this,' Kathryn laughed.

'CIC?' Myra said looking perplexed.

'Yeah. You know, Cat *In* Charge!'

'Oh, I see. Yes. Cat *In* Charge. So I am, dear. Did you hear that, Charles?'

'Meow!' Charles said.

'Doncha love it when a plan starts to come together?' Kathryn said. 'What does that leave us yet to do?'

'The invitations. I'm sure Charles has a program for

that. We have to cover our butts in our private lives and then we have to make arrangements to get to California,' Isabelle said.

'I have to pick up a load of toilet seats, four thousand to be exact, and they have to be in San Francisco by next week. I was supposed to head dead back with a load of carrots, but I can cancel that and pick up a load of lettuce when we're done. You're welcome to drive with me or you can fly and we'll meet up. If Isabelle is staying here, and Nikki has to be here for her court case, that means Julia, Alexis and Yoko have to partner with me.'

'I will drive with you, Kathryn. We can get to know one another. Perhaps I can learn not to be afraid of your dog. Will you have me as your navigator?'

'No!' The single word shot out of Kathryn's mouth so fast her tongue felt like it had been scorched. 'Wait! I didn't mean no you can't go with me. What I meant was . . . Alan always said he was my navigator. That means you can't be my navigator. You can be . . . you can be . . .'

'Your lookout?' Yoko said.

'Yeah. Yeah, lookout is good. No offense, Yoko.'

'None taken, Kathryn. I understand. It is possible we might become friends.'

Anything is possible, Kathryn thought. 'I suppose.' Yoko smiled warmly.

'We need to make reservations if Kathryn's stand-in is to go on vacation. It's still Isabelle, isn't it?' Myra looked at Isabelle who nodded. 'Isabelle can make the reservations and work with Alexis on her disguise. I see a possible problem.'

Nikki stopped writing long enough to look up and say, 'What do you see?'

'Kathryn's truck. Earlier we said when the men try to figure out what happened to them, they would start looking at possibilities and eventually Kathryn's name will come up. If her truck isn't here, and she makes a delivery to San Francisco, that puts her and her truck in California. Even though she is making a legitimate delivery and picking up a legitimate delivery on the way back, it's still going to be a problem.'

Julia jumped in. 'Unless, after the delivery of the . . . ah, toilet seats, she offhandedly tells the people at the delivery site that she's taking two weeks off and going to a resort for a few weeks. Isabelle will make her reservation from San Francisco so she has a ticket to prove that she, aka Kathryn, did indeed leave there, registered at a resort and then flew back to San Francisco and from there back to here under her own name.'

'You need to tell us, Kathryn, how you're going to get fuel on your way to Lone Pine or whatever destination you choose. If you stop along the way, someone is going to remember a woman truck driver. This is all based on the men honing in on you, Kathryn. It may never happen. But, if it does, we need to protect you,' Nikki said.

Kathryn looked up at the platform where Charles was standing next to the computer bank. He nodded. 'I think I can make arrangements for fuel along the way.' He scribbled something on the pad he was holding in his hands.

'Any other questions or details you think we need to discuss?' Nikki asked looking around the table.

Myra stood up. 'I'm going to make us some lunch. Kathryn, you might want to take your dog for a walk. Nikki will assign each of you to a computer where you will order whatever you need shipped to this box number in Washington, DC. Overnight everything. We have a special Visa card for things like this. He'll give you the number. Charles will work on getting the motorcycles. He'll arrange for you to pick them up in San Francisco for your trip north. Talk among yourselves, make it as easy as possible. Pay attention to all the little details people tend to ignore. The little details that can trip you up. I'll come for you when lunch is ready.'

In the foyer, Myra looked up at the chandelier. 'Ah, the power is on again. Light always makes things so much better, don't you think, dear?'

Kathryn held the door open for the dog. He bounded outside. 'I don't know, Myra. It seems I've lived in darkness for so long I can't tell the difference anymore. I don't know what to do. I'm lost. It was like Alan was an extension of myself. I took care of him for so long I don't know what to do with myself. When he was lying there in that . . . that box . . . I got so angry. I screamed and yelled at him for leaving me. He didn't give a good rat's ass about me. He was so ready to die it was pathetic. You know what else, Myra? There was only one other person at Alan's funeral beside myself. A trucker who just happened to be in the area. I wanted to kick him out of the funeral home, but I didn't. The damn funeral director kept coming into the room that was bare of flowers because I didn't even have enough money left to buy a bunch of daisies to put on his casket. I have to deliver those toilet seats and I have to bring back a load of lettuce or I won't be able to pay for his funeral. I had to charge his funeral. Alan must be spinning in his grave. That damn undertaker wanted me to cremate him, said it was cheaper. I couldn't do that because I need to have him in a place where I can . . . I can go. I didn't want him blowing away in the wind. What does that make me, Myra?'

'A grieving widow who loved her husband. I paid for your husband's funeral, Kathryn. You can pay me back someday or not pay me back, it really doesn't matter. I'm so sorry for your loss because I know *exactly* how you feel. When my daughter died, I wanted to die with her. It wasn't until Nikki and I saw Marie Lewellen shoot that man on the courthouse steps that I came to life. That's what I should have done, but I was so grief stricken all I could do was think about my own misery. She had the guts to shoot and kill the man who took her child's life. I can't wait till my case comes up,' Myra said vehemently.

'I'll personally kill the son of a bitch for you, Myra. No parent should have to bury a child. I do thank you for paying for Alan's funeral. I didn't know you had done that. I swear, I'll pay you back.' She opened the door for Murphy.

'Kathryn, you may not be able to go back to trucking if you stay in the Sisterhood. Your time will be required on the cases we have to deal with. Perhaps not every one but on most of them. Charles and I have taken the liberty of fattening up your bank account as well as the other sisters. If we want this project to be successful, we can't have you worrying about food and bills, now can we?'

'Just how rich are you, Myra?' Kathryn asked bluntly. 'If I had a hundred bucks in my bank account, I'd feel rich. Dog food and diesel fuel are expensive.'

'I'm sure they are but you don't have to worry about that anymore. As to how rich I am, I'm not sure. My accountants tell me I'm a billionaire. And all that money comes from making candy. The first batch was made right here in this kitchen on this very table. The old wood burning stove is gone, but I'm sure they poured the candy into trays on this table. Is your dog hungry?'

'He's always hungry. The day I got him I forgot to feed him. He didn't whine or cry or anything. He just waited. I have so many regrets, Myra. I need to know something. I don't know if you have the answer or not but I have to ask. When my case is over, what if I don't feel vindicated? What if . . . I'm not doing this for me, I'm doing it for Alan.'

Myra whirled around. 'Stop right there. You are not doing this for Alan. You are doing it for yourself. You have to admit that to yourself. You cannot hide behind your husband. Make no mistake about that. I think there are many things you need to come to terms with, Kathryn. In your time off, dear, I'll make arrangements for you to talk to a psychiatrist and a grief counselor. I should have done that but I didn't. You're much too young to let all of what went on before destroy your life. Don't even think about saying no. Mothers always know best.'

'Then I won't say no. Do you have any scraps or leftovers I can feed Murphy?'

'I thought you said he ate what you ate. We have turkey, ham and I think there's some roast beef. Fix him a plate and then you can set the table while I make sandwiches and coffee.'

'Myra, do you mind if I ask you something?'

'No, dear, ask me anything you like.'

'Do you think we'll get caught? Do you think there's anyone out there smart enough to figure out what we're doing?'

Myra looked down at the ham platter she was holding. 'I look at it this way, Kathryn. No one's luck holds forever. I'm sure at least one of us will make a mistake along the way. Will it be a serious mistake we can correct or will it be so serious we get caught? I don't know the answer to that. I'm sure there are many smart people out there who, if they had all the facts, would put two and two together. If we're careful, if we stick to our plan, I think we can have a good run. Charles and I have had months to put all this together. There are many safeguards in place. I don't want you to worry about a thing. Charles and I will do the worrying. Besides, that's what you're supposed to do when you get old. Please don't deprive us of this pleasure.'

'OK, Myra.'

'What's wrong with your dog, Kathryn?' Myra asked as the fur on the huge dog's head and back stood on end. He growled, a low menacing sound.

Kathryn whirled around. 'Someone's coming. What should I do?'

Myra ran to the kitchen window. 'It's Jack Emery. He's Nikki's beau. Boyfriend, significant other or whatever you call them these days. Quick, Kathryn, take Murphy and go up the kitchen stairs. Don't let him bark. I'll get rid of Jack. Hurry.' She put her hands to her head as though that would help her to think as she grappled with the knowledge that Jack Emery was going to be knocking on her door any second.

She looked down at the plate on the floor and quickly set it in the sink. She jerked at the refrigerator door handle and jammed the ham platter on to the shelf just as the kitchen doorbell rang.

He was so good looking, Myra wished she was thirty years younger. 'My goodness, Jack, what *are* you doing out here at this time of day? Nikki isn't here. Her car wouldn't start so Charles drove her into town. They're coming to tow it any minute now.' *Please, please, don't let Nikki or Charles come out here. Please.*

'I called her apartment but there was no answer. She's not in the office either.' His tone was so cold, Myra frowned.

'Maybe she went shopping. I am not her keeper, Jack.' *Now he's going to ask about the gate, the cars and Kathryn's truck.* 'Is something wrong?' *Of course there was something wrong.* She steeled herself for the words she knew were coming. 'You caught me just as I was leaving. I'm playing bridge this afternoon. If I hear from Nikki, I'll tell her you drove all the way out here to see her. You should have called and I could have saved you the trip, Jack.'

'Marie Lewellen split. She's gone and she took her family with her. That means you lose the bail money you posted.'

Myra allowed a shocked look to spread across her face as she asked in a horrified voice, 'All of it? The whole million dollars! I refuse to believe that. Are you saying she . . . moved? She wouldn't do that. Where could she possibly go? Maybe the family went on an outing. Disney World is a possibility. Distraction, one last family vacation before the trial, that kind of thing.' *That sounded real good, Myra. Keep your wits about you.*

'She split all right. I'm sure she had some help. No, no one saw anything. She must have left during the heart of the storm. No one was out and about. This is Nik's fault. You never should have posted her bail, Myra. I know Nik talked you into it. This trial was nothing but a farce using the taxpayer's money. It's cut and dried. We could have saved a lot of money by her pleading guilty and cutting a deal.'

'I don't much care for your tone of voice, young man.

This is between you and Nikki. It's my million dollars to lose, not yours, so don't get huffy and righteous with me. And while we're in this talk mode, why did you cheat on my Nikki?'

'What are you talking about? I didn't cheat on Nik?'

'Then who was that redhead you were seen having dinner with?'

'My sister-in-law. Are you sure you don't know where Nik is, Myra?'

'I don't have a clue.'

'Who do all those cars belong to out there?'

'Why are you asking me all these questions, Jack? The cars belong to the canasta girls. It's so weird. None of them would start. Charles had to ferry everyone home. The garages are going to make a fortune today.'

'Who does the rig belong to?'

Myra put her hands on her hips. 'Now, why are you asking me all these questions, Jack? Not that it's any of your business but they delivered some fixtures for the bathrooms upstairs. I'm going to do some remodeling. You know, sinks, tubs, toilets, *toilet seats*, that kind of thing. The driver asked if he could sleep for a few hours since he had to go back on the road. I thought he had left. I wouldn't go near that truck if I were you. The driver has a mean, vicious dog with him. Dogs are better than guns. I saw that on a documentary not too long ago. I don't mean to rush you, Jack, but I have to get ready for my pinochle game.'

'I thought you said you were playing bridge.'

'Did I? Well we never really decide until we sit down. Maybe it's poker today. Then again it might be canasta. Is it important for you to know what kind of game I'm playing?'

'No. I was making conversation, Myra. Was Nik jealous?'

'No. She was . . . pissed off. She has a date with someone named Deverone. Do you know him? She said he had a brain. I really have to go, Jack. I hope you find Marie and her family. I really don't want to lose my million dollars. You people aren't very sharp, are you?'

'Oh, we're sharp all right. That woman had some help. Don't you worry, I'll find her. And the people who helped her. Aiding and abetting a murderer is a serious offense.'

'It certainly is,' Myra said properly horrified.

'Be sure to tell Nik to call me if you hear from her.'

'I'll do that. It was nice seeing you again, Jack. I wish the circumstances weren't so dire. Please let me know if you find Mrs Lewellen. I would like to get my bond back.'

Jack nodded.

Myra scooted over to the kitchen window and crossed her fingers. 'Don't let him go near the truck. Please don't let him go near the truck,' she muttered. He didn't. She didn't realize she was holding her breath until it exploded from her mouth in a loud *swoosh*.

'You can come down now, Kathryn. Hurry. I have to warn Nikki that Jack was here.'

Myra threw the dead bolt on the kitchen door before she headed for the living room and the secret panel. The moment the panel was back in place she rushed to Nikki. 'Jack was just here. He said Marie Lewellen split during the night. He wanted you. I couldn't come to get you so I said Charles had taken you back to town. He's pretty upset, Nikki. He wants you to call him. The redhead was his sister-in-law.'

Myra plopped down on to her chair, breathless with what had just transpired.

'He questioned all the cars and the truck, Nikki.'

'Did he now?'

'Yes. And he didn't believe a word I said. I could see it in his face.'

Six

Nikki gathered up her papers and jammed them into a bright yellow folder she removed from her briefcase. She looked around, honing in on Myra. 'Just for the record, Jack doesn't have a brother. He has a sister who lives in Canada. She comes here quite often. As a matter of fact, I saw her a few weeks ago at the hairdressers. I have to go back to town. The judge probably has a warrant out for me by now. Charles, you're going to have to drive me in keeping with Myra's little . . . fib. I have to CYA. It won't hurt to call a garage to come out and look at *all* the cars. Just shrug and keep saying they wouldn't start. It's called covering your ass, Myra. Jack isn't just sharp, he's razor sharp. Are you getting my point?'

Myra made a mental note to call to have the gate repaired. 'Yes, dear. We'll carry on here. Call me and let me know how things are going. Tell the judge I'm very distraught over Mrs Lewellen and ask him what recourse, if any, I might have? Tell him I send my regards and to say hello to Mavis.'

Nikki snapped the lock on her briefcase. 'Let's hit the road, Charles.' At Myra's inquiring look, she said, pointing to a bright yellow folder with a sticker on the top that said, Quinn Law, 'The Sisterhood stuff is in this file. I'll call you after I speak with the judge . . . and Jack.'

Nikki followed Charles through the secret opening and then waited until she was certain it was closed tightly before she said, 'Did Myra tell the others about Marie Lewellen? I know Julia knows but what about the others?'

'She's going to tell them now,' Charles said reaching for his keys on the hook by the kitchen door.

Ninety minutes later, Nikki marched down the corridor that led to Judge Olsen's office. She gave her name to his secretary and took a seat, her heart fluttering in her chest. She did her best to steel herself for what she knew was coming.

Ruth McIntyre looked over her granny glasses to stare at Nikki. 'The judge has been trying to reach you for hours, Miss Quinn.' The statement clearly implied that her routine as well as Judge Olsen's routine had been upset with their inability to get in touch with her.

'I was in McLean, Mrs McIntyre. It was impossible to leave with the storm and all. The power went out. The phones went down. The battery on my cell phone went dead. I apologize.'

'Mr Emery was here bright and early. The judge and myself were both here at seven.' The glasses on the end of her pointy nose jiggled with indignation.

Nikki eyeballed the cranky secretary and didn't flinch. I'm really sick of this crap, she thought. A tiny smile played around the corners of her mouth. It was downright amazing what a group of women hell-bent on securing justice could do to one's psyche. 'Jack Emery can walk from his apartment to the courthouse, while I, on the other hand, was over an hour away. I'm here now,' she said tightly.

Nikki continued to stare at the judge's secretary. She

absolutely would not allow this woman to intimidate her. She's got to be ninety if she's a day, she thought. She still wore her hair in the style of the 1920s with its side parting and tight finger waves. Pressed powder covered her face and filled the deep trenches alongside her mouth and under her chin. Perfect quarter size circles of rouge were painted dead center on her cheeks. Waxy, salmon colored lipstick crept up to and filled in the deep lines over and under her lips. Even from this distance she could smell her Evening in Paris perfume.

Today the indomitable old bat was wearing a high-necked blouse with a flounce curled around her stringy neck. She knew it was a flounce because Ruth McIntyre said it was a flounce. Myra said she never heard of such a thing but then Myra was a fashion plate and didn't hark to the olden days like Ruth McIntyre did. She was in a time warp, bottom line.

'I have a call into Mr Emery. I believe he's somewhere in the courthouse. I had him paged. You'll just have to wait till he gets here. The judge isn't going to want to go through this mess twice.'

'That's fine, after all it's not like I have anything else to do, Mrs McIntyre,' Nikki responded, her reply courteous but sarcastic. She reached over for a battered and tattered copy of *National Geographic*. She flipped through the curled-back pages and was about to replace the magazine on the table when Jack Emery entered the office.

'It's nice to see you finally made it, counselor,' he said. His tone was velvet, edged with steel.

'It's nice to see your cheery face, too, counselor,' Nikki said taking her cue from his tone of voice. She ached to have him reach for her, to put his arms around her shoulders. It wasn't going to happen. He was pissed and when Jack was pissed you ran as far as you could to get away from him.

'The judge will see you now,' Ruth McIntyre said. 'Remember to be respectful,' she said wagging a long, bony finger at Jack.

'Yes, ma'am,' Jack said.

Nikki ignored the comment and walked through the door ahead of Jack. Her stomach rumbled and she could feel her left eye start to twitch.

She hated this judge. Hated his narrow-minded, sanctimonious attitude toward people and the law. Everything was either black or white. He refused to acknowledge the color gray existed. He went strictly by the book. He should have stood down years ago, but for some unfathomable reason he was still sitting on the bench. She longed for the day when she would see him nodding off in the middle of a trial so she could start a movement to have him retire. Anything. *Anything.*

'Sit down,' he barked. He reminded her of a bulldog. He's his secretary's twin, Nikki thought crazily. The only difference was where she smelled like Evening in Paris, he smelled like Lava soap and vinegar.

They sat. And they waited while the judge eyeballed them over the rim of his glasses. He fixed his beady eyes that watered on Nikki. He jabbed at the air with his index finger. 'You told me Mrs Lewellen was not a flight risk, that she had deep ties to the community. You managed to get her bail. You lied to me, Miss Quinn.'

Determined to maintain her composure, Nikki resisted the urge to stiffen her shoulders. 'No, Your Honor, I did not lie to you. That was what I believed at the time. I had no reason to believe otherwise. These past months as we prepared for trial gave me no indication she would take flight. Furthermore, Your Honor, I only have Mr Emery's word that she absconded. She might have gone to visit someone. It is getting close to the trial date. She might have felt the need to get some space around her.'

Jack turned sideways in his chair. 'She's gone. And they didn't take anything with them either. We went through the house. Their suitcases are still in the closets, their toothbrushes are still in the bathroom, there's food in the refrigerator. They just walked away. That tells me they had to have help.'

'I hope you had a search warrant,' Nikki snapped.

'I had probable cause. That's all I needed,' Jack snapped in return.

'Did you put out an all points, Mr Emery?' the judge asked.

'Yes, Your Honor, we did.'

The judge jammed his finger in Nikki's direction a second time. 'That means Miz Rutledge forfeits the bond she posted. You tell me now, young lady, did you have anything to do with your client's disappearance.'

Nikki's eyes popped wide. Now her shoulders did stiffen. 'Your *Honor*, I did not lift one finger to help my client leave. I didn't even know she was gone until Mr Emery notified Mrs Rutledge, who by the way asked me to ask you if she has any recourse to regain her money. She also said to give her regards to your wife Mavis.'

'Hrumpf,' the judge puffed. He leaned back in his old, cracked, leather chair that fit his lean, bony body like a glove. 'I'm leaving the case on my calendar. I want weekly reports on my desk every Monday morning by seven thirty. File the necessary papers as the occasion arises. I'm not happy with this situation, counselors. Not happy at all.'

'Nor am I,' Nikki said.

'It's appalling,' Jack Emery said.

'It's appalling because you want your face splashed all over the news, Jack. I want to know what your probable cause was. You went out there in the middle of the worst storm ever to hit this state *knowing* Marie was going to take off.' She jabbed her finger at Jack and said, 'It wouldn't surprise me one little bit that you have your fingers in this somewhere. A case like this looks real good to the media. You'll be on the noon news, the six o'clock news and the eleven o'clock news. And your face will be the first one we see when we wake up in the morning to click on the TV. I want to know why and how you thought you had probable cause in the middle of the night or whenever the hell you went out to my client's house. Your Honor, I want an answer!' Nikki bellowed.

Throwing his arms in the air, the judge stood up. 'Both of you, get out of my office and do your fighting somewhere else. Discuss it and settle it.'

'But your honor . . . ?' Nikki pleaded.

The judge's face turned red and then purple.

'We're leaving, we're leaving,' Jack said cupping Nikki's elbow in the palm of his hand to usher her out the door.

'Take your hands off me, you . . . you . . . *prosecutor*.'

'Nik, wait.'

Nikki spun around. 'I'm going to bring you up on charges. Tell me now what your probable cause was . . . You didn't have one, did you? You son of a bitch!'

'Oohh, I love it when you get mad.'

Nikki whirled around, Ruth McIntyre's perfume circling her like a fog. She got in his face and said, 'Read my lips and kiss my ass!'

'There will be none of *that* in this office, ladies and gentlemen. Remove yourselves immediately,' the judge's secretary bleated.

Nikki gave the old bat the evil eye. 'You can kiss my ass, too, lady,' Nikki shot back as she slammed the door behind her. Great, that was just great, Nikki said to herself. I think you just said goodbye to your law career. The thought made her laugh. You already did that when you joined the Sisterhood. Her stomach stopped rumbling and the fluttering in her chest went away with the thought.

'Nik, wait up. C'mon, hold on here. Listen, we need to talk.'

She kept on walking, trying to ignore him.

'Nik, listen to me. Don't go doing something stupid like filing charges. Goddamn it, I did have probable cause. I'm a damn good prosecutor because I have that gut instinct, that extra sense you need to be good in this job. I knew she was waiting for just the right moment. I knew, Nik. I swear to God, I did. I acted on my gut instinct. I was right, too. We both know it. She was looking at a possible life sentence. Hell, if I was in her position, I would have cut and run, too. She killed a man in cold blood. The whole world saw her do it. You want to burn my ass for that, go ahead. I'm going to find her. I will, Nik. If I find out you had anything to do with her taking off, I'll come after you. Whatever went on before won't matter. Now, let's go get a cup of coffee and talk like the educated lawyers we are.'

Nikki smiled and offered up a single digit salute by way of answer. Jack's eyes almost popped out of his head. Other lawyers striding up and down the hallway grinned as Nikki marched away.

That was stupid, Nikki, she said to herself. You just

gave him license to start watching you like a hawk. Stupid, stupid, stupid. Think. You need to think about what you just did and remedy the situation.

And then he was beside her again. Ah, God does work in mysterious ways.

'We really do need to talk, Nik. Come on, let's grab some coffee.'

She knew how to play the game. 'Who was the redhead, Jack?'

'Is *that* what this is all about? You're jealous. I'll be damned,' he said smacking his forehead. 'OK, OK, I see now where that little tantrum came from.' He looked down at his watch. 'The sun will be over the yardarm soon, let's grab a brew at Gilligan's. It's public. Judge Olsen told both of us to talk this out. So, what do you say?'

You dumb schmuck, Nikki almost said aloud. Like I'm really going to fall for this. Whatever it takes to get you off my back. 'All right, Jack. One beer and that's it. I have to go on to the office and I need to get back to the farm to pick up my car. So who was she?'

He answered the question with a question. 'Are you seeing Mike Deverone?'

'I asked you first, Jack.'

He shrugged.

'Fine. You keep your secrets and I'll keep mine. How's that?' She smiled.

'He's a nerd.'

'Everything and everyone is in the eye of the beholder,' Nik said sweetly. 'Actually, Mike is quite charming.' You aren't going to break my heart. I won't allow it, she thought to herself.

Jack huffed and puffed his way across the street. He held the door open. Music blasted outward. Cigarette smoke filled the bar area. Jack headed for the back and a quiet booth.

'Two Buds,' he said to the waitress. 'I've missed you,' he said reaching for her hand. The combination of his good looks, his devastating smile and his resonant voice were almost too much for her.

'Speaking of eyes, Nik, you looked frazzled. Is it the Lewellen case? C'mon, this is me. You can talk to me. Whatever we talk about here is personal, not case related. Let's start over. How are you, Nik? I really missed you.'

'I missed you, too.' That was honest, she said to herself. She had missed him. A lot. 'Where does this leave us, Jack? With Marie gone, if she's really gone, the case will stay open. Possibly forever. I guess we might as well say goodbye now.'

'No, no, no, we'll find her. In a couple of hours her picture will be on the desk of every law officer across the country. Someone, someplace, will recognize her and call the police. That's a given. Possibly a month. Maybe even less.'

'We aren't supposed to discuss the case, Jack. The probable cause bit, yes, but that's it.' Nikki swigged from the bottle and set it down on the little square napkin.

'Are you going to file charges, Nik? Tell me now.'

'You really pissed me off back there in the judge's office, Jack. But, to answer your question, no, probably not. I know a thing or two about gut instinct. I'm sorry to say I never suspected she would do this. You're right about her having help. Are you going to check out her relatives?'

'We're on it. I guess Myra is going to be upset losing all that money.'

'Yes, she's very upset. She's still grieving over Barbara. All she could see was that man killed a mother's child. We're discussing the case, Jack.'

'It's hard not to. Let's talk about us.'

'There is no *us*, Jack. There's just you and me. Separate people. We aren't a couple any longer.'

'That's your fault, Nik. You never should have taken the case. If you hadn't been so damn bullheaded, we wouldn't be sitting here right now at each other's throats.'

'It's not like the guy was innocent. He confessed and his DNA proved it. If it hadn't been for your boss blowing it, the guy would have gotten the death penalty. I asked you to pass on it, Jack, and you said no. If you hadn't been so power hungry to get your name in the papers and your face on the television news, we wouldn't be sitting here. You're right about that.' She drained her beer bottle and plopped it on the table. 'Thanks for the beer. See you around.'

Jack reached for her hand. 'Listen, Nik. I'm hurting here. Can't we make peace? We had a good thing going before this damn case came up. We were the golden couple around town. Now there are days when I can't remember what you look like. Let's just say the hell with everything for the moment and go over to my apartment.'

'Like a quick roll in the sack is going to change things? No thanks, Jack.' Her stomach rolled itself into a tight knot when she saw an ugly look transform his features.

Nikki reached over to retrieve her purse and briefcase. She was so close to Jack's face she could see his five o'clock shadow. 'You put a tail on me and I'll have your ass swinging from the flagpole outside the courthouse, so don't even think about it. I also reserve the right to file those charges we discussed earlier. Fuck up and you'll be begging me to defend you. Of course I'll say no. I don't need another loser of a case in my career. You know, Jack, we could have cut a deal. Ten years, five off with good behavior. Your way it was life and she pays the price for the guy killing her daughter. That's going to stick in my throat forever. By the way, the redhead was your sister. She dyed her hair last month. We met in the beauty shop.' She smiled. 'See ya, sweet cheeks,' she said tweaking his chin.

Jack waved his empty beer bottle at the waitress. While he waited, he whipped out his cell phone to call his assistant. 'Listen to me, Harry, and don't say anything. I want you to put a tail on Nikki Quinn. I want a bug in her car and one in her apartment. I have the key. I know it's illegal, you asshole. Do it anyway. I want one in her office, too. As soon as possible. Don't screw it up, Harry.'

Nikki walked into her law offices on G Street. She'd worked hard to build her firm and she was proud of it. She liked the idea of an all woman law firm and she'd recruited the best of the best. They were winding down now for the day. Time to go home to their families who would welcome them with open arms. All of them, she knew, would be taking home work.

As one they said, 'Tough break, Nik. You couldn't have known so don't go blaming yourself. If you need any of us, just call.'

On her way out the office manager added, 'By the way, the university called. I left the message and a bunch of others on your desk. The mail's there, too, along with a letter that came earlier by special messenger, See ya.'

'Thanks. See you tomorrow.'

Nikki walked into her office and sat down and kicked off her shoes. She eyed the mini bar under the counter and decided another beer was in order. She scooted her swivel chair over to the bar, and uncapped a beer. She slid the chair backward and then propped her feet up on top of the desk. She riffled through the mail. Nothing urgent, nothing even remotely important. She sifted through the pink message slips. Like the mail, there was nothing urgent, nothing even remotely interesting except possibly the message from the university where she taught first year law three days a week. The message read: Call me up till 8:30 here at the office or home later. It was from the dean. She swigged from the bottle as she opened the gray envelope that had been delivered by a messenger.

Nikki took another long pull from the beer as she read it, wondering who she had to thank for it.

Dear Miss Quinn,

I want to thank you for everything you've done on my behalf. I know I let you down and I'm sorry. I wish it didn't have to be this way but I can't abandon my children and my husband. Please don't think too harshly of me.

I know the police will be looking for me but they'll never find us. Never in a million years. I've planned this for a long time. The only thing I wasn't sure of was the time and the place.

I know I have no right to ask this of you, but will you please do me one last favor. Tell the police no one helped me. No one else is involved. Even my husband and kids didn't know until it was the right moment to leave. I left the deed to the house in the cabinet over the sink. You can sell the house and whatever equity is in it, donate it to a victims' rights organization. Please do it in my daughter's name. I don't know if you can explain this to Mrs Rutledge or not. Please try. I know I can never pay her back and I won't even try. Just thank her for caring enough about me to want to help. Maybe someday we'll meet again.'

Marie Lewellen

Nik walked over to the copy machine and slid Marie's letter underneath the cover. She carried the original and the copy back to her desk. She dialed Jack's cell phone number from memory. She didn't bother with amenities. 'I just received a letter from Marie Lewellen. It came by messenger earlier today. Come by *now* and pick it up. I'll have a copy hand delivered in the morning to Judge Olsen. Now, Jack. I'm getting ready to go back to the farm.' She hung up before he had a chance to reply.

Her next call was to the dean at the university. Her gut told her she wasn't going to like whatever he had to say. She identified herself and waited while he inquired about her well-being. 'I'm sorry, Nicole, but the board feels you are too controversial right now. A leave of absence until possibly the next semester was the board's suggestion. At that time we will evaluate—'

'You're firing me, is that it?' she pressed.

'A leave of absence with pay is not firing you, Nicole. We do hope that Mrs Rutledge's . . . The board feels . . .'

Nikki felt the fine hairs on the back of her neck stand up in anger. 'You'll have my resignation first thing in the morning, Dean. I think it's safe to say Mrs Rutledge's endowments will cease first thing in the morning. Have a nice evening, Dean. Like Myra said, everything comes with a price.'

'Hey, Barb! I'm calling your name! Can you hear me? I could use a friend right now.'

'I'm right here, Nik. The dark stuff hit the fan, huh?'

'Yeah and it's splattering in all directions. Can you . . . What I mean is, do you know what's going on or do I have to tell you?'

'I know. So you lost the teaching job. Big deal. Three days a week was three days too many. You were overworked anyway. You were on your way to burnout, girl. It's not like you need the money. What you and the others are doing is so much more important. Concentrate on that and you'll be OK.'

'Jack is on his way over. We had a parting of the ways and I feel . . . awful. You never liked him, did you, Barb?'

'Not really. Maybe that's because I never really got to know him that well. He tries to put you down but you refuse to see it. Maybe I was looking at it all wrong. You are so much smarter than he is. He knows it and resents it. I think he's calculating as well as manipulative, just like you are, Nik.'

'I already figured that out, Barb. I wouldn't put it past him to bug my office and my apartment. Shit, I didn't ask for my key back.'

'He's on his way. Ask him for it. I hear the elevator. See you back at the farm.'

'Yeah, OK.' Am I nuts! she thought to herself. Am I really talking to dead people? I'm breaking the laws I swore to uphold by the dozen. Yeah, I'm nuts.

Jack Emery strode into her office and looked around.

'Really nice digs, Nik. I know I say that every time I come here. Your rent must be half of what I earn in a year.'

No matter what he said, she wasn't going to let him get to her. 'Here, this is your copy. I keep the original. Check it over before you leave. This is the envelope it was delivered in. DBY Messenger Service on K Street. I don't know when they got it or how they got it. Now, I'd like my key back.'

'Your key?' Jack hedged.

'Yeah, you know, the key to my apartment. I want it back and I want it back *now.*'

'I don't think I have it with me. Can I drop it off or mail it?'

'I don't think so, Jack. Let me see your key ring.'

'No.'

'What do you mean, no?'

'If I give you back the key that means it's over. I don't want it to be over. Give me a break here.'

Get the damn key, Nik.

'I want my key. If you don't give it to me, I'm going home to wait for a locksmith. I know one that's open 24/7.'

Jack licked at his lips. 'OK, OK.' He fished in his pants for the keys and removed her key. He tossed it on the desk.

'Do you want a copy of both envelopes?'

'Yes.'

'No problem.'

'How about a beer?'

'Sorry, I'm on my way out. Perhaps another time. Thanks for coming by to pick this up. I knew you'd want to see it right away. I don't want you to accuse me later on of obstructing justice. By the way, the university fired me today.'

To his credit, he looked shocked. 'Jeez, I'm sorry, Nik. I really mean that.'

Nikki bent down to put on her shoes. 'I'll walk down with you.' She was careful to lock the door.

Outside in the cool evening air, they parted company, Nikki walked one way and Jack walked the other way.

Seven

Two days after Nikki's late-night, tearful return to McLean, Myra Rutledge woke from a sound sleep and knew immediately something was wrong. Her motherly instinct was kicking in. She lay quietly a moment, listening. Moonlight filtered through the crack in the drawn draperies. That meant the weather was OK. She couldn't smell smoke. She swung her legs over the side of the bed and slipped into her robe. She looked down at the overlarge digital numbers on the bedside clock: 4:20.

The house was quiet. Charles, night owl that he was, was probably in what they were now calling the War Room. She tiptoed down the back staircase to see Nikki sitting at the table, her head in her hands, a coffee cup in front of her. And she was smoking, something she rarely, if ever, did these days.

'Nikki, what's wrong?' she whispered as she padded into the kitchen.

'Everything and nothing. Want a cigarette?'

The last thing Myra wanted was a cigarette, but she reached for it, stuck it in her mouth and puffed as Nikki held the lighter to the tip. She coughed and sputtered but kept on puffing. 'Talk to me, baby, tell me what's wrong. Just start anywhere,' she said, the cigarette dangling from the corner of her mouth.

Nikki laughed. Myra was game for anything. 'Let me get you some coffee. Maybe I better make some more. I've been sitting here since two o'clock just thinking.'

Her eyes watering from the cigarette smoke, Myra transferred the cigarette to the opposite side of her mouth. Smoke spiraled upward. 'I'm a good listener, dear. Are you having second thoughts about what we're doing?'

Nikki hitched the belt of her bathrobe higher and then yanked it tight. 'In a way, but it's not what you think. It bothers me that Jack came out here and saw the truck and all the cars. That's for starters. At the moment he doesn't have a clue, an inkling of any kind as to what we're doing. He's sharp, though. He's a thinker. No grass grows under his feet. We had this . . . discussion. It wasn't a fight. I wish it had been a fight. I made him give me back the key to my apartment. I had this crazy feeling he might try to bug it. Don't ask me where that thought came from, Myra. I had the locks changed in case he had a duplicate key made.' She plucked at a yellowing leaf on the African Violet sitting on the window sill. Her index finger worked the soil to see if it was dry. It was. She held it under the faucet, wiped off the bottom and set it back on the window sill.

'I think I was blind where he was concerned. He's not who I thought he was, who I wanted him to be. He's power hungry, Myra. He loves being on the tube and in the papers. He is so pissed that Marie split. And rightly so. He won't give up where she's concerned. He's convinced I had something to do with it. Knowing him like I do, I know he has a tail on me. I know he's going to bug my office, my apartment and probably my car. I know this, Myra, because he used to tell me about all the times he'd done it before. Just because we slept together and were planning on getting engaged, won't make one bit of difference. Can you just see the headlines: DA arrests lover and he has tears dripping down his cheeks. Yeah, he'd do that.' She reached for a cup in the cabinet. The minute the coffee stopped perking, she poured a cup for Myra.

'By the way, then the dean fired me. He didn't say, you're fired but that's what it meant. He wanted me to resign so I obliged him and the board.'

'Well, I fixed his wagon. I called him and told him the endowment was now null and void. Let him scurry around somewhere else for his money. He shouldn't have done that to you. I won't tolerate anyone taking advantage of my girl.' Myra puffed furiously on the cigarette, clouds of smoke circling the kitchen. 'What *do* you get out of these things?' she demanded.

'All kinds of health problems. Look, I'm throwing them away,' Nikki said tossing the cigarettes in the trash container under the sink.

Nikki sat down at the table, her hands cupping the mug full of fresh coffee. 'I have to tell you something. You know me better than anyone else in the world. You're the mother I never had. You took me in when I was a little girl and raised me like your own daughter. Do you see a flaw in me? You know, did you ever . . . think maybe I had a screw loose?'

'Good heavens, no. Why are you asking me such a thing?'

'Because . . . because . . . do you believe in spirits, dead people coming back and . . . helping, talking to you?'

'Oh, I see, this farm is finally getting to you, is that it? Dear, there are all kinds of spirits in this old place.

They're floating all around. I've learned to pay them no mind. They're just restless and they did live here. If anything, they've given me a sense of security because I know they're watching out for me. But to answer your other question, no they do not talk to me and no I haven't really seen them. I feel their presence sometimes. It's not a bad thing, dear.'

Nikki bit down on her lip. She'd almost confided in Myra about her little talks with Barbara. She was glad now she'd kept quiet. She sipped from the cup she was holding. She nodded. 'Is everything on schedule, Myra?'

'As Charles says, we are on target. Kathryn and Yoko will be ready to leave for San Francisco as soon as Charles gets his cycle confirmations. Julia is . . . where she needs to be. She'll be doing surgery on her patients at seven o'clock. She'll stay there for three days and then fly back here where they will do what needs to be done at which point she will then fly back to check on her patients, remove the sutures and then fly on to Los Angeles. Isabelle is now working out of the old summer pantry. She's ready to leave on vacation the minute we give her the go ahead. Alexis is in town replenishing her . . . supplies. She'll fly out of Washington the minute everything is settled.'

'Shouldn't I be doing something? I'm pretty much at a loose end, Myra. I turned my caseload over to my partners a few weeks ago. I'm not teaching now. I need something to do.'

'Charles would dearly love it if you would help him. He's dying to show off all he's done to someone who can appreciate his expertise. I would never admit this to Charles or anyone else but that War Room absolutely terrifies me. All those computers, all that knowledge stored on those little squares. The different programs, the lights, the bells and whistles.' She shook her head, her arms flapping every which way.

'Does everyone have a laptop?'

Myra nodded. 'Top of the line, according to Charles. He managed somehow to get what he calls a secure line. It's a line that no one can bug. That means listen in on, dear. I believe they have them in all the big government buildings. It's in case the girls have to call in. From a pay phone of course. Although Charles did give them some kind of new cell phones. He held a class yesterday for two hours teaching them how to use it. It was all Greek to me.'

'After I shower, I'll volunteer my services. Are you wishing your case was first, Myra?'

'I have to be realistic, dear. The man's embassy returned him to China. There are billions of people in China. We could never touch him over there.'

'That's what you think. Myra, the man comes from an influential family. If Charles hasn't already done it, he can get on the information highway and pull him up, in I'd say no less than thirty minutes. I always wanted to see China,' Nikki smiled.

'Are you saying we won't have to wait for him to return here at some point in time?'

'That's what I'm saying, Myra.'

'They never let you out of those Chinese prisons,' Myra said.

'First you have to be caught and be in a prison,' Nikki said smugly. 'That won't happen. Yoko speaks Chinese. Fluently. Kathryn speaks Chinese and seven other languages. She told me she and her husband used to listen to the Berlitz tapes while on the road. She could brush up and be as fluent as Yoko when your time comes. She's also a brown belt. So is Yoko. Alexis can make us all look oriental. The possibilities are endless. Now, you have something to think about and plan while we're on the road or involved in a case.' She gave her a quick hug. 'I'm going to take my shower now.'

Myra beamed, her eyes sparkling. 'Nikki, Jack is so unworthy of you.'

'Tell that to my heart, Myra. From lovers to adversaries.' She shrugged.

'You always tell me everything happens for a reason, Nikki.'

Nikki carried her cup to the sink. 'Myra, is there any way, any way at all, that Jack Emery can find Marie Lewellen and her family?'

'Absolutely none, dear. He will have to get his notoriety from some other case.'

'And they are going to earn a living . . . How?'

'Marie is going to make quilts. She does lovely work. Handmade quilts are outrageously expensive as you know. Mr Lewellen is going to make Shaker furniture and sell it on the Internet. He is so detail oriented. He does magnificent work.'

Nikki burst out laughing. 'And you're going to buy it all up, is that it?'

'Only in the beginning until they get established. I'll donate them all to the church bazaar at Christmas time,' Myra smiled.

'I love you, Myra Rutledge,' Nikki called over her shoulder as she made her way upstairs.

'And I love you, too, dear,' Myra called after her.

* * *

Ten days later, the eighteen-wheeler gobbled up the miles on the interstate as Kathryn Lucas and Yoko Akia sat in companionable silence, the Belgian Malinois nestled between them. They spoke from time to time about the highway, the miles to a gallon the rig got, the scenery and the different loads of merchandise she had transported over the years.

They'd been on the road for two days and still hadn't discussed what had transpired back in Virginia or what would transpire once they got to California.

'We're going to stop at the next road stop, Yoko. Fish some money out of that shoebox. I'll need to fill up and it's time to eat. Remember now, don't do anything to call attention to yourself. This is a straight, legitimate run but we still don't want to give anyone anything to remember.'

'I understand, Kathryn. Three hundred dollars should be sufficient,' she said reaching for the Ferragamo shoebox. She snapped the rubber band back into place and set the box back on the floor. She settled her baseball cap – a gift from Kathryn – more firmly on her head. She looked like a child of thirteen when in fact she was thirty-six.

'Are you going to keep driving, Kathryn? It must be very lonely for you with no one to talk to. I understand you talk to Murphy but he does not answer you back.'

'It is lonely. I've been thinking about a lot of things but I'm so in debt I have to keep doing this. If I live to be a hundred, I'm not sure I can ever get caught up. Alan's medical bills were in the hundreds of thousands of dollars. If I don't drive, I don't know what I'd do. I can't see myself sitting in some engineering office working on something I probably wouldn't like. I've been on the road and in the open too long.

They'd probably fire me after the first week – if I lasted that long.'

Yoko stared out the window. 'What state are we in again?'

'Kansas. We'll be bypassing Oakley soon. There's a decent stop ahead and the food is pretty good. They don't have rice, though, Yoko, and they aren't big on fresh vegetables.'

'It is all right, Kathryn. When in Rome . . .' she giggled.

'You were so worried about being away the other day. How did you manage the time with the nursery? Who's going to take care of it?'

'A family friend. My husband is in California. I hope I do not run into him. He is a cinematographer. A very good one. I, too, am fond of the camera but the nursery pays the bills. I like working with the earth, with flowers and vegetables. I told my husband a fib. I said I had family matters to take care of and he would see me when I finished my business. When I thought about it, I realized it was not a lie. One day it will be my turn to avenge my mother but in order to do that I must be patient and help those who go before me. My husband is very modern in his thinking. He wants me to have my life, my space. We talked about this very much. Many times. It is I who worry. I will not let you down.'

'We got off to a rocky start that first day. I'm sorry.' Kathryn reached across to pat Yoko's arm.

'I understand. We were all jittery not knowing what to expect.'

'What we did, did it turn out the way you wanted?' Kathryn said.

'I think so. I think each of us wanted our case to be first.

I am content to wait my turn. I see now how things will work. Charles appears to have all the right connections. He must have been a very powerful man when he was in service to the British government. I'm happy that you were chosen first, Kathryn. You have carried too many things too long on your shoulders.'

'But you don't approve of the punishment?' It was more of a question than a statement.

'I've had time to think about it and sleep on it. I now agree. However, I think the others are wrong about the men only going after you because the circumstances just happened to be right that night. I think those men have done this many times before. I think they feel confident enough, macho enough, to believe they won't get caught. And they haven't been caught. Until now. I think I will be proved right.'

Kathryn concentrated on the overhead signs on the Interstate. 'That doesn't make me feel any better, Yoko. Nothing will make me feel better until those bastards get what they deserve.'

'It will happen. We must stay calm, centered. You know that from your martial arts teachings. I like this truck,' she said suddenly.

'I can teach you to drive it when this is all over if you like,' Kathryn smiled.

'My legs are far too short. I am content to ride . . . lookout.'

'Shotgun,' Kathryn laughed. Out of the corner of her eye she could see Yoko scratching Murphy behind his ears. The big dog was in seventh heaven with all the attention he was receiving.

'Do you think your dog is starting to like me, Kathryn?'

'Yep. Show Yoko how much you like her, Murphy.'

The Malinois wiggled around, placed his front paws on her lap and barked for her to lower her head so he could lick her chin. 'OK, you're his bud now. It's comforting to know there's someone, even if it's an animal, who will protect you with their life. If I tell you something, Yoko, will you promise never to tell anyone? You have to swear to me.'

Yoko looked across at Kathryn, noticed the grim set of her jaw, the white knuckles on the steering wheel, the stiff set of her shoulders. 'I swear,' she said solemnly.

'I'm afraid. Every time I get in this truck, I'm afraid. I'm afraid to fall asleep for fear someone will break in and attack me. I'm afraid to go to strange places. I'm afraid of everything. I tried to put up a good front for Alan, but he knew. He did everything he could humanly do in his condition to help me, but it wasn't enough. I tried to be so strong and so tough, but it was all an act. I bluster, I say outrageous things just to get me over the bad moments.'

'I know that. We Chinese are an intuitive lot, you know.'

'So I've heard. I'm turning off here. This place is called Sam Slick's Truck Stop. There is no Sam but there is a Samantha. Everyone calls her Sam. She owns the joint. Nice lady. A little hard around the edges but she's good people. Good food, too. She likes to deck out in diamonds and spandex. Beats the hell out of me how she's never been robbed. Course she could be lying by saying they're diamonds when they're really zircons, but who cares. She says she likes to sparkle for the drivers. You'll like her, she's a hoot. The best part, though, is she's got clean showers and bathrooms. That counts when you're on the road. I'll gas up and meet you in the shower, OK?'

'OK, Kathryn.'

An hour and a half later, Kathryn slid into the booth across from Yoko. 'What looks good today?' 'Actually everything *sounds* good.' She pointed to the chalk board over the cash register.

'Kathryn, long time no see,' said a pretty waitress with rough, red hands.

'Hi, Penny. Yes, it's been a while. How's everything? Did you get married?'

'No,' the waitress sighed. 'One of these days. Sam's out back. She'll be real happy to see you. Now, what can I get you?'

'I'll have the fried chicken, mashed potatoes, carrots, French dressing on my salad and cherry pie for desert. Coffee, of course, and I need an order to go for my dog. Three hamburger steaks, double order of carrots, and a cherry pie. Two bottles of water and fill our thermoses.'

'Miss, what will you have?'

'I'll have the carrots and string beans. Cherry pie, apple pie and chocolate cake. Ice cream on all three. Coffee, too,' Yoko said.

'Whoa, little lady, that's some dinner. Did you ever hear of the three food groups?'

'Yes, but I do not care for them. Thank you, my order stands.'

Kathryn was finishing her pie when she felt a poke to her shoulder. 'Move over, *sister*. Hey, hey, what's the matter? You turned white as a ghost. It's me, Sam. Sorry, kid, I didn't mean to spook you.'

'You didn't, Sam. I guess my mind was somewhere else. Sam, this is Yoko. She's riding as far as San Fran with me. It's good to see you.'

Sam Slick was as flashy as her neon establishment.

115

Today she wore her waist-long hair piled high on her head with little ringlets cascading around her ears and down her back. Diamonds winked in her ears. Not just one but three to each lobe. Alan always thought she put her make-up on with a trowel. He was probably right. She had a perfect smile and beautiful teeth that glistened when she talked.

Sam wiggled inside the lemon yellow spandex dress that was two sizes too small. 'We were just talking about you not long ago, Kathryn. Haven't seen you in a while and then one of the boys told me about Alan. I'm real sorry, kid. I didn't know. I would have sent flowers but none of us knew where . . . where you were when it happened. The boys took up a collection. Yeah, yeah, they did. They wanted to, Kathryn. All the girls kicked in, too. You OK, kid?'

'No. It's hard, Sam. Alan was part of me. Now I have a dog, but it's not the same.'

'Of course it isn't the same. I felt like that when Beau passed on. Life didn't have any meaning for a long while, but time has a way of taking care of everything. I know you don't believe that right now but in time you will. Let me get that collection for you. I've been keeping it in the safe all this time.'

'I see what you mean about her being a nice lady,' Yoko said.

'Salt of the earth. Did you see those diamonds on her hands?'

'I felt like putting my sunglasses on,' Yoko giggled.

'Here you go, kid,' Sam said holding out a shoebox that said Pappagalo on the side. We collected over ten grand. You're not going to bawl and embarrass me, are you, Kathryn? If you start howling then I'm going to howl and I don't feel like gluing on these eyelashes again, much less apply my makeup all over again.'

Kathryn struggled for the words but her tongue felt too thick in her mouth. 'I didn't have enough money for flowers and I had to put his funeral on tick. Will you thank everyone for me?'

'No. You just get on that CB and thank them yourself. Listen to me, kid, don't ever be too proud to ask for help. You should have called me.'

Tears burned Kathryn's eyes. 'I wish I had called you. No one came to the funeral except me and a local trucker named Carl Manning. Maybe it was better that way. Thanks, Sam.'

'My pleasure, kid. Drive with the angels. You hear.'

'I hear ya, Sam.'

'Grab the food, Yoko, while I pay the bill. Leave the waitress twenty bucks. She has to hustle here and she's trying to put two kids through college.'

Kathryn paid the bill, fed Murphy and then walked him.

They were back on the highway in less than thirty minutes.

Fifty-two hours later with cat naps of an hour or so along the way, Kathryn pulled the rig alongside the loading dock of the home depot. While her cargo was being unloaded she used the CB to call the dispatcher at the wholesale produce mart. 'Vernon, this is Kathryn Lucas. Listen, I'm sorry but I can't take that load of carrots to Denver for you. My husband passed away and I need to get away for a few days. I'm going to park the rig and get a flight to someplace where I don't know anyone. Four, five days, I'm not sure. I can take some lettuce that way if you want when I get back. If you don't have anything for me on my return, I'll just head home empty. I appreciate your condolences, Vernon. Thanks. I'll call you the minute I get off the plane.'

'Now what?'

'Now we head for Los Angeles and the motel to wait for the others. Call Myra and tell her we're right on schedule. Find out if everyone else will be on time. I really need to get some sleep. I can't wait to fill the tub and take a good, long bubble bath. We have to find a laundromat once we check in. Sometimes motels have a facility but just as often they don't. I suppose we could buy some clothes. We certainly have enough money to do that.'

'I can take care of all that while you sleep, Kathryn. I will call Myra now.'

'Be careful what you say. Just generalities. She'll get the drift. We can't be too careful.'

'Myra, it is Yoko. How are you? We're fine. A little tired. And the others? That's nice to hear. I hope you're well. The weather is very nice. I'll call again when we both have more time. Goodbye.'

'She said everything is whirring. I have to assume she meant everything is in motion and we're all on schedule. It's just a matter of days now, Kathryn. Tell me something, if you could have anything you wanted right now, what would you wish for?' Yoko asked.

'A little cottage somewhere near the water. Maybe a lake or the ocean. A couple of acres so I had some privacy and Murphy could run. A house with a front porch with rocking chairs. A nice kitchen you could eat in. Modern appliances. A pretty bathroom with flowered wallpaper. A walk-in closet. I'd like one of those canopy beds with white lace and one of those big televisions and a chair that would hold both Murphy and me while we watch it.

'I saw some dishes once in a catalog that had tiny little bluebells on them. They were so delicate and so pretty. I'd like to eat off dishes like that instead of Styrofoam. I want big, fluffy pink towels with my initials on them so I know they belong to me. I'd like some bookshelves with lots and lots of books to read on cold winter nights. A fireplace, of course. I'd want a stack of cherry wood because it smells nice when it burns. I want to learn to cook and bake. I love looking at the pictures in cook books.' Kathryn laughed ruefully. 'Since I'll be around eighty when I get out of debt, I doubt I'll ever get a house like that. It's OK to dream, though. I know how Alexis must have felt when she had to sell off her house to pay her legal bills. She told me she owes over two hundred grand in legal bills. I'm right up there with her.'

'I think it's a wonderful dream, Kathryn. I hope it happens for you someday.'

'I hope so, too. If it doesn't, my life won't be ruined. I'm going to get on the CB now and thank all my friends for the . . . you know. Go to sleep, Yoko. You look as tired as I feel.'

'That's a very good idea, Kathryn.'

Kathryn brushed at her eyes as she reached for the CB. 'Hey you guys, this is Big Sis. Anyone out there?'

Eight

The room Myra called the sun room was a beautiful room. It was an addition she'd built on to the old farmhouse the year Barbara and Nikki turned thirteen. The year when sleepovers, scout meetings and parties took up both days of the weekends.

The sun room was always both the girls' favorite room in the entire house. They did their homework at back-to-back desks listening to loud music while the television blared in the corner. Back then there had been a litter box in one corner and a dog bed in another corner. More often than not, Sophie and Bennie could be found snuggled together in the tufted dog bed. Both were gone now, having died of old age. Irreplaceable, Myra had elected to forgo animals in her life because it was too painful when they passed on.

The room was alive with luscious green plants and tall, bushy Fica trees that somehow had managed to survive her two-year hiatus in the nether world. Charles had seen to everything, making sure he fed the plants, trimmed them back and watered them faithfully because he knew how much Myra loved the room.

He knew his beloved Myra was troubled when she lowered her self into one of the His and Her chairs she'd bought for them when the girls moved out. More often

121

than not they dined off trays while they either watched or listened to television.

Life until just recently had been placid, worrisome and boring.

'I think we should get married, Charles,' Myra blurted.

Charles lowered himself into his chair and kicked up the foot rest. 'That's probably the best idea you ever had, Myra. Name the date and I'll be there. Do you want to talk about it or is this just something that came to you in your dreams?'

'I do dream about you, darling. All the time. No, I've been thinking about marriage a lot since we began our little project. The main reason is I love you. I loved you the minute I spotted you standing at the foot of Big Ben. I took your picture, remember? Then we kept meeting up at different places. And . . . husbands and wives can't be forced to testify against each other.'

'That's because I was following you and the others. I was smitten the minute I saw you. I've always loved Americans. I can't say I loved your parents, though. They wanted no part of me. So, you *are* worried about this project.'

'Anxious might be a better way of phrasing it. My parents were not a romantic couple. They were afraid you would coerce me into staying in England. That's why they whisked me back home. The moment they found out I was pregnant they somehow managed to get Andrew Rutledge to make an honest woman of me. I regret that so deeply, Charles. I wish I had been more defiant. Andrew was a kind man but so much older. He didn't have a fun bone in his stodgy body. I felt terrible when he passed on. I tried to find you, to tell you we had a daughter, but you were gone. I grieved for you night and day.

'I still, to this day, remember the moment the call came from your embassy asking all those questions. And then your people came to interview me and to check out our security at the candy plant. They said you would arrive in twelve hours if I agreed to hire you on and never breathe a word of it to anyone. I was so speechless I could only nod. Those twelve hours until you walked through the door were the most anxious hours of my life. You just smiled at me and all those empty years were gone.'

'I never stopped loving you, Myra.' He reached for her hand and squeezed it.

'We should have told Barbara. She grew up and died never knowing you were her father. I regret that. We should have told her, Charles.'

'No. She adored Andrew. You can't rip a child's world out from under them. I think in time she grew to love me as a substitute father. That was good enough for me. We've had a wonderful life, Myra. I have no complaints.'

'Charles, don't you think it strange that Barbara's beau hasn't been in touch with us? The last time I saw him was at her funeral.'

'Ben did call, Myra, many times during that first year but you were so wrapped up in your grief you would just nod when I told you. Ben Gerrity is a fine young man. He moved to New York shortly after . . . after the funeral. He works for Goldman Sachs in the city and is doing well. In fact, he's getting married in June to a lovely young girl who is a physician's assistant to an OBGYN doctor. They're going to live in Bronxville in an old Tudor house.'

'How do you know all this, Charles?' Myra asked in amazement.

Charles smiled. 'I made it my business to find out. It

wasn't that hard. I knew you would eventually get around to asking me and I wanted to have the answers for you.'

'Whatever would I do without you, Charles?'

'For starters, you'd have to learn to cook. You'd muddle through, Myra.'

'You'll be leaving in the morning. Isabelle left on a four o'clock flight. I'll be all alone here worrying myself to death.'

'Nikki will be here, Myra. I gave her enough to do to keep her busy for weeks. She's such a quick study. You tell her once and she grasps it immediately. By the time this first case is over, she will have complete dossiers and files on each case. She's worried about Jack Emery. I have to admit I have some doubts myself where he is concerned. I think it was a stroke of genius on your part, Myra, when you had Isabelle draw up plans for remodeling the bathrooms upstairs. You even took it upon yourself to order four bathtubs, four vanities, four toilets and four shower inserts, not to mention the toilet seats, and store them in the garage. That covers us as far as Jack seeing Kathryn's truck parked here. However, my darling, you goofed up when you said the driver was a man. If he has the presence of mind to run a check on the license plate, he'll know it was a woman. Unless the plate and truck are registered in Alan's name.' He slapped at his forehead. 'How could I have let that get past me? How, Myra?'

'A senior moment?' Myra quipped. 'Nikki's heart is breaking, Charles, and I feel responsible. If it wasn't for Marie Lewellen, Jack might have put the ring on her finger by now.'

'You can't think like that, Myra, nor can you blame yourself. It's better she finds out now how power hungry Jack Emery is and to what lengths he'll go to achieve that power he craves. Sex,' Charles said looking up at the ceiling, 'isn't everything.'

'How long do you think he'll keep at it before he gives up on Marie Lewellen, Charles?'

'People like Jack never give up. The Lewellens are safe where they are in the Amish country. In a month's time they'll adapt. It's as good as it gets, Myra.'

'I'm going to miss you. What should I do while you're all gone? If I just sit here and think, I'll go out of my mind.'

'You could act on what Yoko told you on the phone last night about Kathryn and her little dream house. Or, you can see what you can do about buying back Alexis's house for her. On the other hand, my dear, you could do both. Vienna or Fairfax would be a nice area for Kathryn. You might want to think about possibly going a little further out to Culpepper. More land out that way. I'm not sure about water. If necessary you could build her a pond and put some ducks in it.'

'That's an absolutely brilliant idea, Charles. Do you think I should arrange some surveillance for Mr Emery?'

Charles threw back his head and laughed, a deep belly laugh that made Myra smile. 'I already took care of that. It never ceases to amaze me, Myra. You think like I do. Just when I think I one-upped you, you come up with the same idea a short while later. The reports will be coming in over the computer. Nikki is aware of it.'

'Why did Nikki go back to town this evening? Did she say anything to you, Charles?'

'Nothing other than there were some loose ends at the office. I think she wanted to check for bugs. She said she's going to be staying at the farm for a while. I know that makes you happy.'

'Oh, it does. I understood why she had to move back to town at the time. The commute is long and often she has to be in court very early. Then there was Jack. I hate to see her paying that sky high rent, but she said it's necessary. I wonder if Jack knows or is aware of Nikki's financial situation.'

'When people are in love, they tend to share such things, Myra. I think it's safe to assume, he's well aware of Nikki's holdings. Just like I'm aware of his. The man's got dick, Myra. He's maxed out on his credit cards and has a hard time making his lease payments on his Lexus. Nikki told me a while back that he wanted to move in so they could share the rent. She said no.'

'Thank God,' Myra sighed. She covered her mouth in a delicate yawn. She hoped Charles wouldn't insist on watching one of his favorite western movies.

Charles looked at his watch. 'I think we should head off to bed, Myra. I have an early morning flight. I'm issuing an invitation here, Myra.'

'And I'm accepting it.' Myra twinkled.

Isabelle Flanders adjusted her floppy-brimmed straw hat and dark glasses as she stepped from the taxi. She paid and tipped the driver. She waited another moment until a bell boy loaded her baggage on to a cart to take indoors.

A headache hammered away at the base of her skull and before long she was going to have a full blown migraine. If not a migraine, then one of the hateful visions that had plagued her since the car accident. She didn't know which she hated more.

At the registration desk she handed the desk clerk Kathryn Lucas's Visa card. She scrawled Kathryn's name across the bottom of the reservation form and waited for her key. She mumbled a muffled thank you when the desk clerk slid the key along the marble counter.

She turned to follow the young man and her luggage to her private cottage. She was grateful that the walk was a short one. Later, after the migraine or the vision, she would check out her surroundings. For now she needed water and some aspirin. She tipped the young man and waited for him to leave.

'This is a swinging place, miss. We have five tennis courts, every water sport you can think of, and our nightly entertainment is the best on the island. The Seahorse Pub is where everyone meets in the evening unless they want to go to town. We have a mini-bus if you don't want to walk up and down the hills. The health club is new. The guests like to dance under the stars on the beach terrace. If you need anything, just call the front desk. Enjoy your stay, Miss Lucas.'

'Yes, thank you,' Isabelle said handing him a twenty dollar bill. For sure he would remember Kathryn Lucas as a good tipper.

The moment the door closed behind the young man, Isabelle ripped off the sunglasses and straw hat. She rummaged in her purse for her aspirin bottle and gulped down four of them with a swig of water from the mini bar. She walked out on to the lanai and sat down under the shade of an umbrella. She closed her eyes and waited. Either the headache would come on with force or the vision would appear behind her closed lids.

Why couldn't she be normal like everyone else? Because Rosemary Wexler ruined your life, that's why. She could hardly wait till it was her turn so she could rip Rosemary's face to shreds.

It came then in the form of jagged streaks of bright light

and then the grainy, gray forms that were people she didn't recognize. This time she saw a car and something that looked like a black marble. The gray form was sticking the marble under the bumper of a BMW. And then it was over. She rubbed at the corners of her eye with the knuckle of her index finger. For some reason her eyes always teared after a vision.

The first time it happened, she'd gone to a doctor thinking she'd torn her retina or perhaps something worse. The eye doctor had sent her to have her arteries tested saying possibly a piece of plaque might have broken off. The test had shown nothing wrong at which point the doctor told her not to worry, her eyes were fine. When she'd gone back a second, a third and then a fourth time, the doctor had lost patience with her and referred her to another doctor who basically said the same thing. There was nothing wrong with her eyes.

The day she'd ruled out all medical reasons, she'd gone to the library and researched all things paranormal. She saw things, but she never knew what they meant. She never recognized the places or the gray, grainy people that appeared before her. Until today. She'd seen the BMW clearly. What did it mean?

With nothing on her hands but time, Isabelle headed for the shower. It was such a relief to take off the heavy, red wig.

An hour later, dressed in shorts, T-shirt and sandals, her own hair piled high on her head, the straw hat on top, Isabelle fixed herself a stiff drink and carried it back out to the lanai.

As she sipped at the scotch and soda, she wondered if she would be able to enjoy herself on this brief vacation. It had been six years since she'd gone on a vacation and even then the vacation had only been a four-day long weekend with a man she thought she would one day marry. After the accident, he'd disappeared the way her business and bank account had disappeared. A businessman in town, he didn't want to be tainted with the same brush. 'Screw you, Steve Whitmore!' she muttered. 'And screw all the rest of you who believed Rosemary Wexler's line of bullshit. My day is coming!'

Isabelle downed the remains of her drink and eyed the mini bar through the sliding glass doors. Why not? She was on vacation. She could use a little glow in her life even if it came from alcohol.

'Shit! Damn it, I was supposed to call Myra.' Her movements were frantic as she fumbled through her purse for the cell phone Charles had given her. She screwed her face into a grimace as she tried to remember Charles's instructions. She finally got it on the third try. 'Hi,' she said.

'Well hi yourself,' Myra replied.

'I should have called sooner but it's incredibly hot here and I wanted to take a shower. I had . . . one of those . . . you know.'

'And?'

'I saw something I never saw before. A detail. In the past, everything was always vague, unidentifiable. This time I saw a man doing something with a marble to a BMW. I don't know what it means since I don't know anyone who has a BMW. I can't seem to function after . . . afterward.'

'I think you do know someone who has a BMW. I want you to think about it when we hang up. Sit back and relax. Eventually it will come to you. I assume then you had no problems with your flight or check-in?'

'None at all. It's very hot here. Oh, I said that, didn't I?'

'Yes. Everything is fine here. Enjoy your vacation . . . Kathryn.'

Isabelle walked over to the mini bar and reached for one of the small bottles of Dewars. She replenished her glass and headed back to the lanai.

She leaned back and closed her eyes. Whom did she know with a BMW? No one. Before Rosemary, she knew several clients who tooled around town in BMWs. Somehow she didn't think that was what Myra meant. Then what did she mean? She brought a mental picture of the parked cars in Myra's oversized, circular driveway to the forefront of her mind. Pricey cars. The truck. Her car. The square black car, what was it? A BMW. Whose? The Jag belonged to Alexis and was leased. The Bentley was Julia's. The Benz belonged to Yoko and her husband. The Honda Civic was hers. Who did that leave? Nikki! Nikki drove a BMW. OK, who was the man and what was he doing with a black marble?

Maybe it wasn't a black marble at all. Maybe it just looked like a black marble. As hard as she tried, nothing else would surface. Maybe after a few more drinks she'd be relaxed enough that she might remember something else.

Dusk settled quickly and before she knew it, the world outside her villa turned midnight black. She looked around as little lights sprang to life on the lanai casting everything in a dim yellowish light that was not unpleasing.

She probably should think about ordering something from the kitchen. She'd only had a bagel in the airport but that was over twelve hours ago. Maybe some popcorn shrimp, a garden salad, a slice of cake and then she could go to sleep. In the morning she could think about BMWs, black marbles and Rosemary.

Back in Virginia, Myra paced up and down her bedroom as she tried to figure out what Isabelle's vision really meant. She longed for Charles who would undoubtedly have the answer. What did a black marble have to do with Nikki's car? Was someone putting them in her gas tank? Someone! My foot, someone. More than likely that someone was Jack Emery. Would he do something that stupid and hope Nikki would call him for a ride or ask him to pick her up? Myra shook her head. That scenario was too ridiculous for words.

She wished now that she had paid more attention to all the spy shows Charles was so addicted to, particularly the reruns of *I Spy* and *Mission Impossible*. That had been Charles's world for so long. A wry smile tugged at the corners of her mouth. He was certainly in his element now with everything he'd conjured up.

Myra looked at the little clock on her night stand. Nikki would probably still be awake. Should she call her or shouldn't she? If anything happened to Nikki, she would never forgive herself. She didn't stop to think. She picked up the phone and punched out the numbers to Nikki's unlisted number. She would be so relieved when Nikki moved back to the farm tomorrow.

'Hello, darling, how are you? I just called to say good night. Did you finish everything you wanted to get done? I would like it very much if you'd do me a favor, Nikki. Ever since that ugly storm my car has been acting up. I was wondering if you'd lease a car and drive it out here tomorrow. It doesn't matter what kind of car you get. Either Charles or I will drive you back to the city to get your own car. By the way, dear, do you remember my friend, the one who *sees* things. She called earlier and said she had a vision. I don't believe in things like that, do you? I feel just plain old silly even mentioning it. She always makes me nervous when she brings things like that up. Sleep tight, dear. I appreciate you doing this for me.'

Myra stared down at the phone. Was she being silly? Would Nikki pick up on her subtle warning? Of course she would, Nikki was smart. She sat down on the edge of the bed. She thought about the conversation she'd just had with Nikki. It sounded like something out of a bad spy novel. And yet, Charles had seemed more than a little worried about Jack Emery. His words were, it's better to be safe than sorry.

Now that she was here alone in her bedroom, the house silent, she could give way to her fears with no one the wiser. She wondered what she would look like in an orange jumpsuit with shackles on her wrists and ankles. She flinched at the thought. On visiting days, Nikki would cry and Charles would wring his hands. She'd probably cry herself and say something noble like, if I had it to do over again, I'd still do it.

Charles said everything he'd done was foolproof. Nikki backed him up. And yet, things had a way of going wrong at the last moment. A dog could upset a foolproof plan, a stranger could appear out of nowhere and screw things up. The human element was one thing impossible to foresee.

If she kept this up, she was going to go out of her mind. She needed to do something and she needed to do it now. What? She looked around as though searching for her answer. She saw it in the pile of comforters on the chaise lounge in the corner of the room. She didn't stop to think. She gathered them up and in the hall she tossed them to the foot of the steps. She peered over the bannister to see if they fell on top of one another. They had. A second later she was sliding down the staircase, whooping in glee. She hit the bottom none the worse for wear. She might do it again later on or in the morning. She smacked her hands together in satisfaction.

She rubbed at her rump as she made her way into the living room. Earlier, she'd closed the heavy draperies. Now all she had to do was close the pocket doors leading into the dining room and she could enter the War Room. Charles had scared the *bejesus* out of her by saying there were high-powered binoculars that allowed a person to see almost a mile away. Then he'd gone on to tell her about the night vision goggles. 'Keep the damn drapes and doors closed, Myra,' were his exact words.

She certainly was getting an education. It was exhilarating and scary at the same time.

The panel closed silently. Myra walked around the room, marveling at the high-tech world that was now part of the old farmhouse. She looked up at one wall and saw Chris Matthews talking to Mike Barnacle on MSNBC. She looked across the room to see Larry King talking to a psychic named John Edwards.

She walked up the two steps that led to the platform where the bank of computers rested under the big screen closed-circuit monitor. She counted down, three, four, five, six. All had little envelopes twirling about signifying that there was incoming email. They were probably from Charles's people. That's how she thought of them, Charles's people. Without those people working in the background, she wouldn't be standing here now, nor would she be obstructing justice and breaking the law.

Myra sat down at the round table and thought about King Arthur. 'We're sort of like that,' she muttered. Her hands started to shake so she sat on them as she watched Larry King and John Edwards. He was so young to be a psychic, but then Isabelle was young, too. Isabelle just saw things and didn't know what they meant. John Edwards seemed to know what everything meant. She wondered what would happen if she called into the show. Damn, why not?

She was out of the War Room in a flash and in the kitchen dialing the number of the show. She waited while she was put on hold. Her hands started twitching again so she tilted the phone on her shoulder and ear and sat on her hands. She almost fainted when she heard Larry King say, 'Go ahead, McLean, Virginia.'

Go ahead. What did that mean? Talk. Yes, she was supposed to say something. 'Good evening Mr King and Mr Edwards. I was wondering if you could tell anything by just my voice. You know, pick up on what's going on in my life. I'm not sure I believe in things like this but I keep an open mind.'

'Can you tell anything by talking to this woman, John?' King asked.

'I see a high impact hit-and-run accident. Did this happen in China? I see Chinese lettering of some kind. I see turmoil and a lot of activity surrounding you. I also see danger. You have to be careful. You like chocolate eclairs. I see you eating three at one time. I see you surrounded by motorcycles? Does that have any special meaning to you?'

Myra slammed down the phone so hard it bounced off

the kitchen counter. She put her head between her legs until her head cleared and she could breathe normally. She was off the chair a second later, opening the refrigerator. She reached for Charles's vodka and took a healthy gulp. Then she took a second one. She debated about a third swallow and put the bottle back on the top shelf.

If she told Charles he would say she was on the phone long enough for someone to analyze her voice. 'Oh God, oh God, oh God.' Well, she wouldn't tell Charles. Maybe she should tell Nikki. God, no! She could ask her tomorrow if Jack Emery ever watched Larry King. Probably not on a Saturday night. Young, good-looking, power hungry men like Jack Emery didn't sit home on Saturday night watching Larry King. Did they? She would have to be careful when she quizzed Nikki in the morning.

There was no way she was going to be able to sleep now. Charles could always buy another bottle of vodka. Right now she needed it more. Maybe she could just stick a straw in the bottle and drink it that way so she could sit on her shaking hands.

'There's no fool like an old fool,' she muttered over and over as she guzzled from the bottle because she didn't have any straws.

Charles said she was to stay alert in case he needed her. Her shoulders slumped. She wondered when she'd gotten two of everything in the kitchen.

'Some CIA, I am,' she muttered as she tottered to the living room, the portable phone in her hand. The cat in charge slumped down on the sofa and was out like a light in two seconds flat.

Nine

Kathryn Lucas looked around at the sleazy surroundings of the motel room she shared with Yoko. It was so depressing she wanted to bolt outside to where the air was clean and fresh. Alexis, Julia and Charles had registered earlier and were three doors down from her room. She sat down and sipped at the cold coffee in the styrofoam cup she'd gotten earlier in the coffee shop. The harried waitress at the register hadn't bothered to even look at her when she paid for the coffee and tea for Yoko.

Sometime during the night, Charles had attached a decal to both sides of the truck. A green and yellow sign that said in bold hunter green letters, TSOJ Manufacturing. Pictures of different types of scales dotted the long banner. Kathryn found herself giggling at what the sign represented. The Scales of Justice. On the sliding door in the back, he'd added another sign in bright red letters that said 'How's My Driving?'. Underneath was a toll free number to call should anyone have a complaint. The truck also now sported a Colorado license plate.

Just a while ago, Charles had said in his best spy voice, 'All systems are a go.' She would have preferred him to say, 'Time to rock and roll, kids.' She blinked at the thought. That would have been movie dialogue.

This was the *real thing*. She shivered inside her lightweight jacket.

'How much longer, Kathryn?' Yoko asked.

'Not long. Alexis is making the others up. She's going to do me first and then I'm off to see Dr Clark Wagstaff to have him check my receding gums. From there I'm going to see the CPA Samuel La Fond. Then it's on to Sidney Lee to buy some insurance. I should be back here no later than eleven thirty. The run doesn't kick off till one o'clock. We're OK time-wise.'

'Are you sure, Kathryn, this is a wise thing you're doing by going to see those three men?'

Kathryn shrugged. 'Wise or not, I'm doing it. I want to look into their eyes. I might have one bad moment when Wagstaff sticks his fingers in my mouth, but I'll think of more pleasant things while he's doing that. Just knowing tomorrow he will be minus his balls will give me a rosy glow.'

It was Yoko's turn to shrug. 'Don't forget your street map.'

There was no knock on the door, no indication anyone was near. Kathryn looked up to see Alexis opening a huge travel case. 'You're first, Kathryn. Drag that chair into the bathroom where the light is better. Why do all motels think their customers like orange and brown drapes and spreads?' she grumbled as she opened pots and jars.

Twenty minutes later she stood back to view her handiwork. She clapped her hands in approval. 'You look like an older version of Britney Spears, Kathryn.'

Kathryn looked in the mirror. Alexis was right. She laughed aloud.

'Hey, I could have made you look like Madeline Albright or Janet Reno. Just don't stand under any bright lights. This will hold up for about ten hours. We'll need to do a patch job when we get to Lone Pine. Change into that yellow suit and you're good to go, girl. 'Yoko, let's get started on your boob job. So, what size to you want to be?'

'I want breasts like grapefruits,' Yoko said smartly.

'You're too small-boned. How about big oranges?'

'Big oranges are good,' Yoko giggled.

'Then let's get started,'

Minutes later, Kathryn cleared her throat. 'What do you think?'

'My God, Kathryn, you look beautiful,' Alexis said in awe. 'That suit fits you like a glove. Nice shape, girl. I like those shoes, too. Ah, a Chanel bag. I like that. You should get dressed up more often. Here's the keys to my rental car,' she said tossing the keys. Kathryn reached up and caught them in mid air.

'Thank Myra. She bought everything. I always liked yellow. It's . . . never mind. I'll see you when I see you. I have the map, Yoko. Stop worrying. Good luck with the boob job.'

Being the first appointment of the day guaranteed Kathryn an early departure to keep her other two appointments on time. She looked around the waiting room that was just like all dentist's waiting rooms. The paintings on the wall were imitation Chagal but not unpleasing to the eye. The magazines were crisp and clean, the plants thick and luxurious. The burgundy leather chairs were actually comfortable, the lighting just right.

She zipped through the form attached to a clipboard and scribbled a name at the bottom. She handed it to the receptionist just as a dental assistant called her name.

'Dr Wagstaff will see you now, Miss Lowenstein.'
Kathryn followed the young woman down the hallway
to a room with a large number three attached to the
door. 'Doctor is reviewing your chart. It will be just a
few minutes.'

She was young. They were always young. Either the
doctor favored young blood or young, fresh out of school
girls didn't demand high salaries. She settled herself in the
chair, allowed the sweet young thing to attach a paper bib
around her neck. She crossed her ankles and stared at the
tips of her Bruno Magli shoes.

She knew he was in the room even though the door
had opened silently. She had one brief moment of blind
panic when he came to stand next to the chair. His scent
was all too familiar, so familiar she wanted to bolt out
of the chair. She gripped the arms so tight her knuckles
grew white.

'A little tense, are we, Miss Lowenstein? I don't bite.
That was a joke. You were supposed to laugh, Miss
Lowenstein. Do you mind if I call you Monica?'

Kathryn shook her head as she stared up at him. He
was handsome, there was no doubt about that. And he
had perfect teeth that he liked to show off. All the better
to bite you with, you son of a bitch. She stared up into his
eyes wondering what he was thinking. She saw absolutely
no recognition. She smiled.

Out of the corner of her eye she watched him pull on
latex gloves. To protect himself from her. She almost lost
it then. He was afraid of her mouth but he hadn't been
afraid to stick his dick in her without a condom. Hatred
bubbled within.

'Do you have a fear of dentists, Monica?'

Kathryn struggled to take a deep breath. 'Yes.'

'I'll make this as painless as possible, I promise,' he said in a reassuring voice. He flashed his pearly whites for her benefit. Kathryn almost gagged.

I promise you pain like you can't imagine, Kathryn thought to herself.

'Did I miss something here? One minute you're petrified and the next minute you're smiling. Share with me.'

'My mother always said to think about something pleasant and wonderful in the dentist's chair. I was trying to do that.'

'I see.' Clearly he didn't see at all. 'Open wide and say ahhhh.' Kathryn obliged.

'I don't see a problem, Monica,' Wagstaff said poking and picking at her gums and tooth line. 'I would recommend using a water pic if you aren't already using one and flossing regularly. Your gums look sound and healthy to me. I'd like to see you in a year.' He stepped back and allowed his assistant to tilt the chair into its upright position.

The doctor stripped off his gloves and handed them to his assistant, but not before he patted her rear end. Kathryn watched as she swished her way to the waste container, a smile on her face.

As she was ripping at the paper bib she noticed a framed newspaper article on the wall. She stared at it for long seconds: Dr Wagstaff astride his Indian, his feet planted firmly on the ground, staring straight into the camera. She pointed to the picture. 'Do you ride, Doctor?'

'A bit. I organized a bike run for a local group here to raise money for underprivileged children. I'm proud to say we raised close to fifty thousand dollars. A lot of children benefited from that run with dental and medical care. As a matter of fact, this afternoon I'm doing a benefit ride to aid a battered women's group. Do you ride?'

Kathryn flipped her Britney Spears hairdo and said, 'Goodness no. I don't even ride a bicycle.'

'Now that I see you standing up, you remind me of someone.'

Kathryn waved her hand. 'People say that to me all the time. Just this morning someone told me I look like Britney Spears's older sister,' Kathryn said forcing a laugh.

Wagstaff shrugged. 'See my receptionist and we can make an appointment for you in, let's say, ten months or you can call us around that time. It's up to you.'

'That's fine. Thanks. I feel a lot better knowing my gums aren't receding.'

'It happens to the best of us,' the Doctor said over his shoulder as he walked out of the room.

'Isn't he wonderful?' the young assistant gushed. 'He's always doing something for someone. He's very civic minded. He usually makes the newspapers once a month at the very least. It was nice meeting you, Miss Lowenstein.'

'Likewise,' Kathryn said as she opened her wallet to pay for the visit. She raised her eyes at the hundred and fifty dollar office visit. She plunked down three fifty dollar bills and waited for her receipt. 'I'll call when it's time for an appointment. I travel a lot and I'm not sure where I'll be in ten months.' She stuck the receipt into the pocket of her yellow jacket and left the office.

Outside in the fresh, spring air, Kathryn took deep gulping breaths until she felt calm enough to head for the parking lot and Alexis's rental car, where she shed the yellow jacket in favor of a green one. She replaced the Britney Spears wig with an Orphan Annie one. Next stop, Samuel La Fond, CPA.

According to Charles's map, La Fond had a suite of offices two blocks west. She looked at her watch. She might be a tad early but so what.

Kathryn stepped into the CPA offices and fought with herself not to turn around and leave. On display, between the coffee table and two dark-blue chairs was an Indian motorcycle with a sign on it that said DO NOT TOUCH. DO NOT CLIMB ON THIS MOTOR-CYCLE. The walls were peppered with framed pictures and newspaper articles attesting to Samuel La Fond's prowess on cycles. The only magazines on the table were biker magazines and biker catalogs. She wondered if he would set his pickled balls on one of the shelves when they arrived in the mail. She felt chagrined to see that there wasn't a life-size wax figure of Samuel La Fond. She asked the receptionist.

'Mr La Fond thought that would be a bit much. Mr La Fond is free now. Walk through the door on the right.'

He was a big man. Real big. He lumbered when he got up from behind his desk to walk around it to shake her hand. He'd put on a good twelve pounds, maybe fifteen, since that night in the parking lot of the Starlite Cafe. He had big hands. Those same hands had squeezed her breasts so hard the bruises stayed with her a full month.

'I need a good accountant for my business. A friend recommended you. I didn't bring anything with me on this trip, but if you are taking on new clients, I would be happy to schedule a second appointment. I have an S Corporation and my corporate year ends the end of September. We have plenty of time the way I see it.'

'What type of business are you in, Miss Walley?'

'Bottle caps,' Kathryn said looking around at the pictures of La Fond in various poses on different motorcycles. The room was like a shrine. To himself.

'Bottle caps?' La Fond echoed.

'Bottle caps. All bottles need caps. It started as a hobby. You know, collecting all kinds of caps. Then one day I got this idea and voila! The company was born. We grossed twenty-three million last year and we're still in the embryo stage.'

La Fond sat up straighter in his chair, his eyes greedy. 'I can always find the time to take on a budding enterprise. Why don't we schedule you for, let's see,' he said scanning his appointment book, 'a month from today. How does ten thirty sound?'

'That sounds just fine.' She ran her fingers through her Orphan Annie wig and smiled. A month from now, you bastard, you won't even remember this office exists. You'll be too sore to even look at those pictures on the wall. She was up and off her chair with her hand on the doorknob before he could plough his way across the room. She noticed for the first time that his belly hung over his belt. There was no way she was shaking hands with this grotesque man. She walked through the doorway. 'Is there a charge for this visit?'

'No. I'll bill you when you come in the next time. Have my secretary write out an appointment card for you. Actually, my secretary is my wife. I don't have to pay her a salary.' He laughed to show how smart he thought that was.

'Really,' Kathryn said as she eyeballed the woman behind the desk. Myra would know to the penny what the woman paid for her outfit. Straight off Rodeo drive if she was any judge. No shortage of money here, she thought.

144

She stared at the woman's cleavage as she accepted the appointment card she handed her.

Two down and one to go.

In the car, she removed the green jacket and slipped into a long, burnt orange lightweight coat. She looked around the parking lot to see if anyone was watching before she peeled off the Orphan Annie wig and plopped on a Tina Turner job. She adjusted the spiky, straw-like hair in the rear-view mirror. She actually looked good in it. She hummed the words to *Proud Mary* as she turned on the ignition. Before she drove out of the parking lot, she scanned the map in her lap.

She had to backtrack and then head north for one mile where she was supposed to make a left at the third traffic light. She closed her eyes, memorized the route and the landmarks. 'OK, Mr Sidney Lee, you're next.'

Thirty-five minutes later she was seated across from Sidney Lee. It was hard to tell what he was other than a fast talking insurance salesman. Swanky offices with rich paneling, good furniture, Berber carpeting, trophies out the kazoo and a clear polished desk. She couldn't make up her mind what nationality he was. He could have passed for Greek, Italian or maybe even Jewish. But there was a cast to his eyes that said he had some kind of oriental blood in him. He went by the name Lee instead of Sid or Sidney. Strange.

'So, Miss Darnell, my secretary tells me you want to buy some insurance. Well, you came to the right place. What exactly do you have in mind?'

'Well, Mr Lee, the past five years have been extremely lucrative for my partner and myself. My accountants tell me I need to buy some Keyman insurance for both my partner and myself. He suggested ten million each to protect us should anything happen down the road. We each one want to take . . . oh, excuse me, my phone is ringing.'

Her heart beating trip-hammer fast, Kathryn realized something somewhere had gone awry. Her hello was cautious. She listened.

'Kathryn, Sidney Lee is not going on the ride. He canceled out this morning at eight fifteen. He didn't give a reason.' Kathryn continued to listen to Charles's instructions, her heart fluttering in her chest. She turned away so Sidney Lee couldn't see her frightened expression.

'Really, Shelia. I'm at Mr Lee's office now. Yes, I can do that. If you can hold on a minute, I'll ask him. Mr Lee, by any chance can you find the time in the next ninety minutes to meet with my partner and myself at the Beverly Hills Hotel? We really want to sign off on these policies today since Shelia is leaving tonight for England. We can pay the whole year's premium right up front and you can send the paperwork to our office later on. Do you see a problem?'

Lee's face contorted making him look more oriental. 'Ninety minutes isn't much time. Today doesn't seem to be my day. I had to cancel a motorcycle benefit run for charity today.'

Kathryn watched him knowing greed would win out in the end. She felt like cheering when he nodded. 'Yes, Mr Lee can make it.' She frowned as she listened to Charles telling her he'd reserved a villa under the name of Shelia Star, supposedly her partner's name. Villa Number Eleven. 'Tell him you can do business on the patio if he balks at being in a room with two women which I don't think he will but just in case. Now listen carefully to the directions in case he wants to follow you. Try to avoid that scenario.'

She listened, her trucker's mind filing the directions in her mind. 'I'll see you in a bit. Yes, I'll tell him.'

Kathryn fought the urge to spit on the piece of scum standing in front of her. 'I have a stop to make before I head back to the hotel. I'll meet you there. We're in Villa Eleven. We can sit on the patio and have drinks and lunch if you have the time. I hope that's satisfactory. I really have to run.' She carried his stunned expression with her all the way down in the elevator and out to the car. 'Now what the hell am I supposed to do? Which disguise do I get into now?' She drove slowly, her heart slamming back and forth inside her chest. What were they going to do at the Beverly Hills Hotel? Charles said everyone would be there. Did that include Charles, too? Who was going to register?

The first glitch.

They were waiting for her when she knocked on the door. Her feet literally left the ground as Julia pulled her inside. In a million years she never would have recognized any of them, especially Charles.

'Time is your enemies, ladies. Alexis is going to be your business partner, Shelia Star. Julia and Yoko will wait in the bedroom until he's under the drug. I can't stay here with you. You're on your own.'

'He's going to remember me, Charles. I sat across from him. If he goes to the police, he can describe—'

'A bad Tina Turner wannabe. This is not a catastrophe. It's a little glitch and we've taken care of it. Admirably, if I do say so,' Charles preened. 'I'll see you in Lone Pine in, let's say, seven hours or so, depending on traffic.'

'Julia, slip this into his drink,' Charles said handing

over a small vial he extracted from his leather jacket. 'This will knock him out for eight to twelve hours. You only need one to two drops.'

'This is Rohypnol! It's illegal to use this in the United States. Where did you get this, Charles?' Julia demanded.

'The black market is a wonderful thing. You're worried about illegalities! Get over it. Good luck.' Charles walked out through the door on to the patio.

The women looked at one another just as a knock sounded on the door. Julia and Yoko ran to the bedroom and closed the door. Kathryn opened the door and ushered in the insurance man. 'I suggest we get right to it, Mr Lee. You don't have to explain the policies, we're both familiar with them. Our accountants explained them to us in great detail. We'll just sign the forms and write you out a check. Here, have a nice cold bottle of ice tea,' Kathryn said holding out a bottle of Snapple.

'I don't like tea,' Lee said rummaging in his briefcase for the forms he wanted.

'Coke or Pepsi?' Kathryn asked.

'I don't like sweet drinks.'

Alexis sucked on her bottom lip. 'Are you saying you don't want to toast us for buying all this insurance with you? That's not very business-like. How often does this kind of deal fall into your lap? I like to socialize with the people I do business with. I was really looking forward to drinks and a nice leisurely lunch. I know this is a rush for you, but time is money in our business.'

'By the way, what *is* your business? I'm sorry. It's just that I promised my fiancée I would take her to a polo match. She's never been to one. I'm running late as it is. I'll have some bottled water if you feel a toast is in order. This is where you sign off on each of these forms. You know at some point, you'll both have to take a physical but don't worry about that. I know a doctor who will make sure you both pass.'

'I don't know why, but I thought you were a married man with a bunch of kids. Most insurance men are married. At least the ones I know,' Kathryn said reaching inside the mini bar for a bottle of Evian water. She turned around and opened the bottle of Rohypnol and added four drops before she put the cap back on the bottle. She was unscrewing it for his benefit when she handed the bottle to Lee. She handed Alexis a coke and she kept the Snapple. 'I thought I told you what our business was back in the office. We make tea bags. You know those little paper things that have tea in them. We make the paper and the tag that hangs out of your tea cup.'

'I thought Lipton made those.'

'See, that's what everyone thinks. We're the brains and they get all the credit. Where should I sign? Oh, I see, right under Shelia's name. Shelia, honey, write this nice man a check so he can go on to his polo match. You didn't say, do you have children, Mr Lee?'

'Four. Two boys and two girls. They live with their mother.' Lee reached for the check, looked at it and almost swooned. He slipped it into a zippered compartment in his briefcase.

'Drink up,' Alexis said.

Both women watched as Lee took a healthy swallow of the water in the bottle.

'Shoot!' Alexis said. 'We didn't make a toast. Let's see, I think we should make a toast to Mr Lee and a long profitable business association.' She brought the coke bottle to her lips and watched as Lee tried to bring the bottle to his own lips. He took a long gulp before he slid to the floor.

'OK, we're in business!' Kathryn shouted. 'Batten down. Close the drapes and slide those dead bolts home but make sure you hang out the Do Not Disturb sign. 'Julia, he didn't drink all the water. What if he doesn't have enough in him? I put in four drops thinking we'd be lucky if he drank a quarter of it.'

'I'll put a little on his tongue. Get the shower curtain and all the towels you can find. Strip him down girls while I get ready.'

This was her moment. The day she'd waited for for seven long years. Kathryn stood on the sidelines as Alexis and Yoko hustled. She saw them spread the shower curtain and a thick, white towel on the coffee table. She watched as they pulled off his shoes, his trousers and his boxer shorts and then hefted him on to the coffee table.

Julia pulled a paper surgical mask across her face. She pulled on two pairs of latex gloves. She saw the others watching her. 'Just in case of a nick. I don't want to kill him considering my condition.'

Kathryn ripped at the Tina Turner wig and threw it across the room. 'The table's too low, Julia.'

Julia dropped to her knees. She fixed her gaze on Kathryn. 'This isn't exactly brain surgery. I can do it on my knees. Now, how do you want this done? The way it would be done in a hospital or do you want it quick and dirty?'

'Quick and dirty,' Kathryn said clearly. Alexis' thumb shot upward. Yoko gave her new breasts a boost and nodded.

'You got it. I'll talk my way through it so you know what's happening.' Julia reached for her scalpel. 'I'm lifting his penis so I can cut into the scrotum. I am going to deliver it through the scrotum sac. You might not want to watch as this can be extremely bloody even though I'm going to clamp it off. I'm going to tie off the arteries with silk sutures. Then I'm going to tie a square knot around the cord. Just so you know, inside the cord is where the blood vessels are and epididymis inside the cord. I'm tying it off. I'm going to staple the skin to bring it back together. This might be a good time to rinse out that Snapple bottle, Kathryn and fill it with formaldehyde. It's in my bag.'

Kathryn's hands shook and then steadied as Julia dropped what looked like two balls into the bottle. 'Screw the lid on tight,' Julia said.

Five minutes later, Sidney Lee, insurance broker, was bandaged and being dressed.

'No more testosterone or erections for you, Mr Sidney Lee,' Julia said as she ripped off the surgical mask and stripped off the latex gloves.

'It was so . . . quick.'

'Here today and gone tomorrow,' Alexis said.

'I told you it wasn't brain surgery. I could have done it with my eyes closed. I want to do that to my husband so bad I can taste the feeling,' Julia said with energy. 'OK, we need to sweep this place clean. Everyone put on a pair of latex gloves and go over this entire place and clean anything you might have touched. The toilet handle, the refrigerator, the door knobs. Keep the gloves on until we get in the car. Yoko, take the check out of his briefcase along with the insurance forms. Stuff them in my medical bag. Bundle up the bloody towels and shower curtain and put them in a pillow case. Leave a hundred dollar bill on the dresser to pay for the towels, shower curtain and pillow case. Leave another ten dollars for the drinks. Wipe the bills clean. It might be a good idea to wash them first. Kathryn, get your wig and put it on.'

'What . . . what should I do with . . . this?' Kathryn asked holding up the Snapple bottle.

'Stick it in your coat pocket for now. Mark it somehow so you know who they belong to.'

'I don't need to mark it,' Kathryn said.

'OK, we're outta here,' Alexis said taking one last look around the villa to see if they had forgotten anything. 'Everyone, just stop for a minute. Think carefully. Did you touch anything you forgot to clean? My fingerprints are on file. Yours are too, Kathryn. Julia, how about you?'

'Mine are on file, too. Yoko?'

'Yes, mine are also. I will go around one more time to be sure. The knob on the outside door needs to be wiped clean,' she said breathlessly.

'Good thinking,' Kathryn said clapping her on the back. Two out the back door, Yoko and I go out the front. We'll meet you at the motel.'

'Do not look at him again, Kathryn. It will serve no purpose.'

'How did . . . ?'

'I know. Come, we must hurry. We want to look normal so we should smile and talk as we make our way to the car.'

'So, you're liking your new boobs, huh?'

'Yes, I do.'

'You know, Julia could give you a *real* set if you want, I bet. You could surprise your husband for his birthday or something.'

'I will think on the matter. It is not out of the question.'

Kathryn laughed all the way to the car, Sidney Lee's nuts bobbing up and down inside the Snapple bottle.

*   *   *

Myra was out the kitchen door the minute she heard Nikki's car crunch to a stop.

'Myra, what the hell is going on? You scared me half to death last night with that phone call,' Nikki said climbing out of the car.

'I know, I know. Isabelle called and she had this . . . this vision. She saw someone bending over a car sticking a black marble in it. It was a BMW. You drive a BMW. I was too befuddled last night to think clearly, but now I've had time to think, I think someone planted a . . . a bug in your car. That's why I didn't want you to drive it. I hope I'm just being paranoid.' She looked upwards. 'It's going to pour any minute now. Come along, dear.'

Nikki tossed her purse and briefcase on to one of the kitchen chairs. 'Do you have any fresh coffee? I just rolled out of bed, leased the car and here I am. I never feel alive until I've had two cups of coffee. He wouldn't dare. Jack wouldn't do that to me. Yes, he would,' she said, her shoulders slumping.

Myra set a cup of coffee in front of her. 'Isabelle always said her visions were never defined, but this time she said she clearly saw the letters BMW. It might mean something and again it might not. You need to have a mechanic check out your car, Nikki.'

'And if I do find out there's a bug in it, how can I prove Jack did it? I can't. I'll call a mechanic I know when I finish my coffee. Anything new?'

Myra sat down with a thump. 'I think that depends on what you mean by new.' She recounted the evening's events up until the moment she fell asleep on the sofa. 'Does Jack watch the Larry King show? I rather thought Saturday nights he would be out either with his friends or on a date with you. Does he, Nikki?' Myra asked wringing her hands as she paced the kitchen.

'Sometimes he watches the show. Even if he was home, I doubt he would have stayed tuned once he realized the show was about the paranormal. He doesn't believe in stuff like that. The answer is, I don't know.'

Myra continued to pace. 'It's eleven o'clock here so that means it's eight in California. Kathryn will be getting ready to visit those . . . those men. I imagine we'll hear something from Charles via email in the next few hours. There seems to be a lot of email waiting. The envelopes were twirling all over the place last night. I didn't want to touch anything. You know how Charles is with his electronic gadgetry.'

Nikki nodded as she tipped her chair back and reached for the phone. She squeezed her eyes shut as she tried to recall the number for Tony's Auto Body shop.

'Tony, it's Nikki Quinn. Listen, I have a tremendous favor to ask of you. No, no, you don't owe me anything because of your sister Angela. She paid the bill. I'm perfectly willing to pay you for your time. I'm working on this case and I have reason to believe someone bugged my car. It's parked on the street outside my apartment building. I keep a spare key under the right fender in a magnet box. Can you go there now and check it out? You can? Thanks. Now listen, I want you to write this down. Jack Emery is the person I want you to deliver it to if you do find something. I'll give you his address. Assuming you find something, when you give it to him make sure he understands it's from me. I owe you, Tony. You'll call me right away if you find something.'

'Right away, Miss Quinn.'

Her eyes miserable, Nikki got up to put her cup in

the sink. 'It should take less than a half hour till Tony calls back. I'm going to scoot upstairs and take a quick shower.'

Her own eyes miserable, Myra said, 'I'll sit by the phone, dear.'

Ten

Sweat dripped down Jack Emery's body as he ran at five mph on the treadmill in his apartment. He was breathing hard, his arms swinging at his sides. Ten more minutes and he would have run ten full miles on the machine, a gift from Nikki on his last birthday. He picked up his pace and did the last ten minutes at six mph, the machine quivering under his fast-paced run.

Six minutes flat, he thought in satisfaction when he yanked at the safety cord and hopped off. He wiped the perspiration running down his face with the sweatband on his wrist and headed for the shower. The doorbell rang just as he turned on the hot water. He gave his boxers a hitch and marched out to the door. He looked through the peep hole and frowned. The guy looked familiar but he couldn't immediately place his face. He yanked open the door.

'Are you Jack Emery?'

Jack pointed to his name over the doorbell. 'Yeah.'

'Then I guess this is for you. Nikki Quinn said I should hand deliver it to you. Have a nice day.'

Jack looked at the electronic device in his hand. Son of a bitch! He slammed the door shut and marched back into the bathroom. For sure his relationship with Nikki was over. He cursed again using words he hadn't used since his days on the street back in the Bronx.

In the shower he lathered up and let the hot, steamy water beat on his naked body. He stared into the steamy mirror as he dried off. If Nikki found the bug it meant she was searching for it. Which in turn had to mean she had something to hide. His gut told him she was up to her eyeballs in Marie Lewellen's disappearance. And rich-as-sin Myra Rutledge was probably right there with her, aiding and abetting. 'You fucking rich people think you can get away with anything,' he muttered as he stomped his way into the bedroom to get dressed.

Now he had to go to the office so he could get to the bottom of Nikki's involvement. He had to satisfy himself one way or the other where she was concerned. The ironic thing was, Nikki would have done the same thing if she'd been in his position even though she wouldn't admit it.

He was pulling on his socks when the phone rang. He debated a moment before he threw himself across the bed and picked up the phone from the nightstand. 'Emery, here,' he barked.

'By any chance do you mean Asshole Emery?' Nikki asked coldly. 'You bugged my goddamn car, Jack. I want to know why?'

Jack clenched his teeth so hard he thought he heard his jaw crack. 'Because you're up to your neck in Lewellen's disappearance that's why and we both know it. Don't take that as an admission of guilt, Nik. I'm going to find her. Then I'm going to prove you and Myra are responsible. Yeah, old Myra said the words but she doesn't care about losing the mil. All she wanted to do that day was to get me the hell out of her house. Do you two think I just fell off the watermelon truck?'

'I'm going to fry your ass for this, Jack.'

Jack looked around his messy apartment trying to

compare it to Nikki's bright airy apartment that was neat as a pin. It even smelled clean and good, like Nikki herself. His apartment was shabby, dreary and messy with beer bottles, pizza cartons, dirty socks and smelly sneakers all over the place. He closed his eyes. 'Not if I fry yours first. Is that what you called to tell me?'

'Myra asked me to file a lawsuit against your department. She said you were supposed to be guarding Marie Lewellen and you let her get away. She's suing for the full million and she wants another million for the angst and fear she's going through. I'll file the suit on Monday. You want to settle now?'

'Up yours.'

'Better tell your boss. I'll hand deliver the subpoena. Hey, look at it this way, you bastard, you'll get your picture in the paper. Don't call me, I'll call you.'

Jack slammed the phone back into the cradle, his face murderous. She'd do it, too. Christ, now what was he supposed to do?

In less than thirty minutes he was storming into his office, the same murderous look still riding his features. He sat down at the computer and started to bang at the keys.

The scrap of paper torn from his notebook was alongside the computer. He typed in the license plate number of the eighteen-wheeler parked at Myra Rutledge's house. They could have spirited the Lewellens away in the truck in the middle of the storm and no one would have been the wiser.

Alan Stephen Lucas. Born August 3, 1958. Address: PO Box 206 Vienna, Virginia. He stared down at the Social Security number and wrote it on a yellow pad of paper. He tapped in more numbers using the department code to allow him access to the Social Security files. He blinked and then knuckled his eyes. *Deceased.* The guy was dead! He cleared the screen and typed in the number again. Alan Stephen Lucas was just as dead as he was a minute ago.

Did the guy sell the truck? Was it part of his estate? Why was someone still driving the truck and using Lucas's license plates? He scanned the screen to see the date of death. Not quite five weeks ago. Time enough to take care of details like selling the truck or changing the plates. Lucas wasn't old, so that had to mean there was a widow someplace. Then again, maybe the guy was divorced.

Jack yanked at his desk drawer and pulled out a well thumbed booklet with access codes to the different government agencies. He typed in Bureau of Vital Statistics and then the name Alan Stephen Lucas and waited while the screen processed his request to be faxed a copy of Lucas's death certificate. He cursed ripely when he realized he would have to wait for Monday for the fax. He typed the words in capital letters RUSH, TOP PRIORITY.

Did truckers belong to unions? He didn't know. He tapped and punched for the next hour until he came up with Local 233 in Roanoke, Virginia. Even if he sent an email, he'd probably have to wait for Monday for a response. Instead he copied down the telephone number and called it. He waited through eleven rings before a gruff voice came on the line and said, 'Yeah, what's your poison?'

Must be trucker lingo. Jack identified himself and said, 'I'm trying to locate Alan Lucas. Do you know how I can reach him or his wife?'

'Alan died a while back. I don't know where his wife is. She's probably on the road somewhere. She's the one that drives the rig. Alan was disabled. Why do you want him?'

Jack ignored the question and asked one of his own. 'Do you know how I can reach his wife?'

'Do I sound like a private secretary, mister? Send her a letter.'

'Yeah, thanks for your help.' Wise ass.

It wasn't such a ridiculous idea. He cleared the screen, brought up Word and typed a message saying it was imperative Kathryn get in touch with him as soon as possible. He filed the message in his personal file folder but not before he printed it out. He scribbled the address on the official stationery, ran it through the postage meter and dropped it in the mail basket.

He flexed his fingers. He was on to something. He could feel it. His nose twitched like a rabbit's. 'Let's try the Bentley next,' he muttered.

Jack stripped off his jacket and rolled up his sleeves. What the hell, with Nikki temporarily out of the picture, he didn't have anything better to do on a Saturday afternoon.

Winston Bugle frowned as he hung up the phone. He didn't have any use for cops or district attorneys. He reached for the CB and said, 'This is Bugle Beagle out here. Anyone listening? I need to get a message to Big Sis. All you ears pay attention now, you hear. Tell her some DA called from the district asking questions. Saw on the ID he was calling from DC. Keep trying Big Sis until she responds. Have her call me. Over an' out.'

Myra made no pretense of not listening to Nikki's conversation with Jack Emery. The moment she hung up the phone she said, 'Was that wise, Nikki? Won't that just fuel things with Jack?'

'It's called CYA. Covering your ass. I know Jack. From time to time he has to be reined in. I told you he's sharp. He's one of the best and for that I can't fault him. He has that old prosecutor instinct. I respect that. He really does hate injustice and he hates defense attorneys of which I am one. He says they catch the bad guys and people like me make sure they walk away clean. We had a lot of fights about it. He'll shave a corner here or there to get the job done. His instinct has always been right on the money. He knows in his gut we had something to do with Marie's disappearance. He just can't prove it. Yet.

'I'll bet you fifty dollars, if I call him at the office, he'll answer. The minute he hung up from me he high-tailed it there. He'll stay there all day, through the night and all day tomorrow if he's on to something. All I did was throw a bone he now has to deal with. It was just to throw him off stride a little. The man has a single-minded purpose in life. Shit, Myra, I can't even hold that against him. He came off the streets of New York. He worked his way through college and law school. No one helped him. He's where he is because he earned his way.

'Yes, he's power hungry. He likes being on the news and he likes getting his picture taken with the mayor and the police commissioner. So do a lot of other guys. He just made it happen for himself. He's pretty much going by the book and we're the ones that threw the book out.'

'That was a sterling testimonial, Nikki. That tells me you are still very much in love with Jack Emery.'

'I'll get over it.'

'What do you think he'll do next, dear?'

Nikki threw her hands in the air. 'My guess would

be the first thing he'll do is change his underwear. The word lawsuit against the office is a really dirty word. He's going to have to call the DA, the mayor and then the police commissioner. Then he's going to go to the office and run those license plates if he did take them down. Jack has a mind like a steel trap. There is one good thing about Jack in regard to his career and his profession, though. He keeps everything to himself, you know, close to his vest. Part of it is that wild ambition of his and it's also part of the thoroughness of him. What that means, Myra, is, he gets all his ducks in a row first and then he pounces.'

Myra sat down with a thump. She longed for Charles as she struggled for the right words. 'Dear, does that mean we'll have to . . . *take him out?*'

Nikki doubled over laughing at the expression on Myra's face. She sobered almost instantly. 'It just might come to that, Myra.'

'Last minute check, sisters,' Alexis said as she jammed her canvas bags in the trunk of her car. 'Yoko, you're driving my car and I'm riding with Kathryn. That's in keeping with what Kathryn told Miz Slick, that you were just going as far as San Francisco.'

'Is everything wiped clean?' Julia asked.

Yoko adjusted the blue bandanna wrapped around her forehead, allowing her long silky hair to cascade down her back. 'I wiped everything twice,' she said peeling off the latex gloves. 'With alcohol from Julia's bag,' she added as an after thought.

'We all checked out using the automatic room check-out. That's all taken care of. Yoko, did you clean off the remote controls?'

'Yes, I did, Kathryn. We're leaving the rooms cleaner than they were when we checked in.'

Kathryn looked at the Tag watch on her wrist. It did everything but talk to her. 'Time to rock and roll, sisters.'

Yoko giggled. 'Stay close behind me and whatever you do, don't speed or call attention to yourself. We're driving straight through so there won't be any stops. Anyone have to use the bathroom?'

'No, mother,' Julia grinned.

'Let's go. We're only forty-five minutes behind schedule. Jeez, wait a minute! Did someone remember to go to home depot to pick up the folding table? We do need an operating table.'

'That was my job. I picked it up on my way in. It's in the trunk. I took it out of the box so my fingerprints are all over it. If we leave it somewhere, remind me to wipe it clean,' Julia said.

'I'll remember, Julia,' Yoko said. She slid into the car. The moment she put the key in the ignition, she let out a yelp. 'This is a stick shift! I do not know how to drive with gears.'

'Oh shit!' Alexis said. 'It was the only one left. OK, OK, crash five-minute course. See this, it's in the shape of an H. Middle is neutral. Low, straight up is second, down to neutral, top of the H is reverse and then down again to third which is high and you cruise in high. You need to use both feet. At the same time, Yoko. You ease up on the clutch, feed a little gas and shift, low to second to third. Each time you have to use the clutch. For each gear, Yoko. You got that? Now, if you hit a hill, you have to be careful or you'll slide backward. Julia, you drive behind her in case that happens. That way she'll only slide into you. Try it, Yoko, once around the parking lot. If you get stuck drive in first. We'll keep an eye on you.'

'I'd say this is a glitch. That's two so far. Three if you actually count the surgery,' Kathryn said grimly. She watched with the others as the Ford Taurus bucked and chugged forward, then backward and came to a dead stop a foot from them. The car bucked and stalled.

'I think I got it. I'm ready. I can do this, Kathryn.'

'I know you can, kiddo. Think wagon train, sisters,' Kathryn said hoisting herself up into the cab. She started to sing, 'Rolling, rolling, rolling . . .'

They were ninety minutes out of Los Angeles when Kathryn's personal cell phone rang.

'You can't answer it, Kathryn. You're supposed to be in Bermuda,' Alexis said.

'I know. It's a Nextel. It takes messages. When it stops ringing, I'll talk you through the process to retrieve the message.'

'I have the same phone. I know how to do it. It's Sam Slick,' Alexis said raising her eyebrows. 'She said Bugle Beagel wants you to call him. Some district attorney wants to talk to you asap. She said you have his number. The call is out to all truckers to give you the message. She said, if you need her, to call anytime of the day or night. That's it,' Alexis said hitting the power button to turn off the cell phone.

'Glitch number four. Call Myra on the cell phone Charles gave you. Repeat the conversation verbatim. I'm sure the DA is the one that came to the house. He ran a check on the license plate. I knew it. I had a bad feeling the day he came to Myra's house. Easy, Murphy, easy. It's OK,' she said to the big dog who picked up on the anxiousness in her voice.

Five minutes later, Alexis looked across at Kathryn as she absent-mindedly scratched Murphy's head. The big dog did everything but purr. 'Nikki answered and she said to stick to the plan and to call the DA when you get back from Bermuda. I think Isabelle's flight gets in around eleven Monday morning. I'd say call him around twelve thirty. Time for you to pick up the truck and your load of produce.'

'Is this glitch four or is it five?'

'Four with a hangnail. It's OK, Kathryn. I like this dog of yours. The truth is, I like everyone involved in this little venture. Yoko is growing on me. I saw Julia smile and once she actually laughed out loud. That has to be hard with a death sentence hanging over your head. Nikki is the one I feel sorry for. Isabelle is so sweet and so very tired. Myra and Charles are just loves. You're OK, too, Kathryn. Being in prison had to be a piece of cake compared to what you lived through.'

'What was it like, Alexis?'

'It was bad. The worst thing of all was when the doors clanged shut. The word clang is so perfect. Every damn time they shut, I wanted to jump out of my skin. I never close doors where I live now. Even the bathroom door stays open. I don't know if I'll ever get over that feeling. Everything smelled like Clorox. The food was inedible. The bed was hard as a rock. Roaches were everywhere. Everything was on a schedule. I made a lot of friends after I learned how to play the game. The whole time I was in there I didn't have one visitor nor did I get one piece of mail. Most days I didn't know what day it was unless someone told me.

'The worst thing, though, was the nightmares. I lived with the trial and the outcome every day since I was

166

convicted. I spent a year in prison so those slime balls could cheat old people and fatten up their bank accounts. One of them even has a yacht now. I swear it's as big as an ocean liner.

'My real name is Ann Marie Wilkinson, not Alexis Thorne and I damn well want it back. I was born with it and it belongs to me.' Tears rolled down her cheeks. Murphy reared up and licked them away.

'We'll get your name back. Don't you worry about that,' Kathryn said with such vehemence Alexis bolted upright. 'And I'm going to see to it that you get that ocean liner providing you take me and Murphy on a cruise.'

'You sound like my champion, Kathryn. Thank you for that.'

'We're all in this together.'

'You know what I think, Kathryn. I think we make one kick-ass team. I sure as hell wouldn't want to go up against us. Would you? Are you anxious about tonight?'

'A little. I was pretty calm when Julia did her number back there in the motel. He should be waking up just about the time we get to Lone Pine.'

'What'd you do with his nuts?'

'They're swishing around back there in Alan's old lunch box. It's in the back by his wheelchair.'

Alexis burst out laughing. 'How did you feel, Kathryn?'

'Angry. Bitter. Numb. It was all so surreal. I knew it was happening and I knew I was watching and being a part of it, but only half of me was there. The other half of me was back there in the parking lot of the Starlite Cafe where it happened. He was the one that sodomized me. If his nuts hadn't been in that Snapple bottle, I would have jammed that bottle up his butt.'

'Spoken like a true woman. One down, two to go. By

midnight or thereabouts, you will be vindicated. Don't for one minute think you're going to magically find closure, Kathryn, because it ain't gonna happen. People always say they're looking for closure for this or that. It really doesn't happen. You can't erase the memory. It will always be with you. The best you can hope for is some kind of vindication,' Alexis said as she settled herself more comfortably in the seat. 'Just knowing there are three men out there walking around without their balls is going to please me no end.'

'Yeah, me, too. Do you suppose they'll walk differently, kind of duck-like?' Kathryn asked.

Alexis went off into a peal of laughter. 'They won't have to worry about which side to put *them* on anymore. I heard Tom Jones the singer used to pad his pants on stage so people would think he had a big set. I wonder if that was true.'

Kathryn laughed until her sides hurt.

An hour later, Alexis said, 'Kathryn, do you see what I see?'

'It's the bikers. Oh, God, there's Charles in the lead. What should I do? Pass them or stay behind?' Kathryn dithered. 'Shit, they're straightening out, that means they want me to pass them. Don't look at them, Alexis.'

'Hey, chickee baby,' one of the bikers shouted as Kathryn pressed down on the gas pedal.

Alexis hung her head out the window and looked at Charles as Kathryn roared past the trail of motorcycles. 'Yo, dude!' she shouted. Charles waved, a wicked grin on his face.

'You had to do that, didn't you?'

'Yeah,' Alexis laughed. 'I've been called a lot of things in my time, but no one ever called me chickee baby before.

They must have stopped for food or something. They had at least a fifty minute head start on us. Before you can ask, I think there's thirty-seven of them. That's counting Charles.'

'How far from ground zero?'

'Three hours, maybe a little less.'

'I'm counting the minutes,' Alexis said as she snuggled up with Murphy.

Jack Emery rubbed at his tired eyes before he picked up the stack of papers he'd printed out. They could just be papers or they could be something else. He leaned back in his swivel chair as he scanned the sheets in his hand. Why would women in their late thirties and early forties be playing bridge with an old lady like Myra Rutledge? Just by scanning the sheets he'd say they were more likely to belong to the same gym as Nikki. But they were at Myra's.

A prominent plastic surgeon married to a United States senator might conceivably travel in the same circles as mega rich Myra Rutledge. He'd seen the power couple's picture in the paper at least once a week, but never with Myra Rutledge. The name Isabelle Flanders tickled his brain but he couldn't remember where he'd heard it before. Alexis Thorne and Yoko Akia. And of course, Nikki. Myra said Nikki wasn't there the day he'd walked through the ruptured gates. He frowned. Were the others in the house that day? If they were, he hadn't seen them. But that didn't have to mean anything. They could have been in the sun room or the dining room. So what? People like Myra Rutledge played cards in the middle of the day and served little finger sandwiches to the card players.

Unlike his mother who cleaned houses for a living

to support his three sisters and two younger brothers while he was growing up. She had always been home to make dinner and then left again to clean offices at night. She didn't know the first thing about playing cards. She probably didn't know how to make little finger sandwiches either. He thought about the hundred bucks a week he kicked in along with his siblings to pay for her care in a nursing home. He didn't begrudge the money because he loved his mother, he just wished she would get better, but he knew no one recovered from Alzheimer's disease. His eyes burned when he remembered his last visit to the nursing home. For one minute she'd recognized him and called him Jackie. A second later she asked him if he was a doctor.

No, his mother didn't know people like Myra Rutledge.

He wondered now if he should have told Nikki about his mother. Why hadn't he? Why did he let her think he didn't know how to manage money, that he was a playboy DA? Why did he trade in his old reliable Honda for the Lexus and was now sucking wind because the lease payments were strangling him? Why did he do half the things he'd done where Nikki was concerned? Had he in some cockamamie way been trying to compete with the life she had with Myra Rutledge? Did he think a boy from the Bronx couldn't measure up? Yeah, yeah, that's exactly what he thought.

He looked at his watch. If he drove like hell, he could make the nursing home before they got his mother ready for bed. Maybe she'd call him Jackie again tonight. Maybe.

Jack made it to Winchester just in time before lockdown. He waved to the charge nurse and made a beeline down the hall to his mother's room. He stood in the doorway watching her for a full minute before he said, 'Hi, Mom!'

'Is your mother here, young man? I don't see her.'

'I guess she left,' Jack said perching on the side of the bed. 'Would you like some company?'

'I always like company. Where is your mother?'

'She's close by. She won't mind if I stay and talk with you for a little bit.'

'I think I'm a mother. Do you know if I am, young man?'

'I think you're probably the best mother in the whole world. I'm Jack. Do you remember me? Think, Mom. Jesus, I miss you. I try to get out here as often as I can but I can't always make it. I just want you to know I try.'

'Are you going to cry, Jackie? It hurts me to see you cry, honey. No one is here so if you want to cry it's OK. I won't tell anyone.'

Jack dropped to his knees. He almost swooned when his mother stroked his hair and started to hum under her breath, 'Hush little baby . . .' He blubbered like a baby and didn't know why.

Jack moved away and reached for his mother's hands. 'Mom, listen to me. If someone killed Betty Ann, what would you do?'

'Who's Betty Ann?'

'Your daughter, Mom. My sister. What would you do if someone killed her?'

'If I was Betty Ann's mother, I would kill them. What would you do, young man?'

'I tried to stop her, Mom, but I wasn't quick enough. I was going to send her to jail for the rest of her life but she skipped out on me. I have to find her.'

The woman sitting in the chair grappled with what he

was saying. Jack watched as she struggled to find words to respond. 'Mothers are . . . They love . . . They protect their young with their lives. Are you sure I'm a mother? Do you need someone to protect you, young man? I think I can do that. Tell me what you want me to do.'

Jack leaned over and kissed her cheek. 'Just say Good night, Jackie. The nurse is here to get you ready for bed.'

'Good night, Jackie.'

'I'll see you next week, Mom.'

'If I see your mom I'll tell her I saw you. What's your name again?'

'Jack Emery. Good night, Mom.'

Outside in the hall he heard his mother say, 'That young man lost his mother. It's so sad.'

Outside in the warm spring night, Jack sat down on an iron bench in the little courtyard by the main entrance. He bit down hard on his lip, his shoulders shaking. He didn't see the tall thin man walk through the doorway nor was he aware of him when he made his exit half an hour later. He did see the man talking on his cell phone when he passed his car on his way to the Lexus that was parked three aisles away.

In the kitchen at the farmhouse in McLean, Myra Rutledge listened to the voice on the other end of the phone, her jaw dropping as she absorbed what the private detective was telling her. She hung up the phone and looked around for Nikki. She called out.

'I'm upstairs, Myra. Do you want me to come down?'

'If you don't mind, dear. I have something to tell you.'

'I hope it's something good,' Nikki said coming down the steps.

'It's sad, Nikki. Sit down and I'll tell you. It's about Jack Emery.'

Nikki's face turned white. 'Did something happen to him?'

'No, no, nothing like that.' She still loves him, Myra thought.

'That was the private detective Charles hired to . . . ah . . . tail Jack.'

'What?'

'It seemed like the right thing to do at the time, dear. I think you'll be glad we did when I tell you what I just found out.'

'This better be good, Myra.'

Eleven

Kathryn slowed the truck to a mere crawl as she instructed Alexis to look for a side road that Charles had marked on the map in red pencil. 'We should be coming up to it any minute now. We've passed all the landmarks he told us to watch out for. What does it say on the margin, Alexis?'

'You're to drive one and one half miles down the road and park once you turn off. He said there is a huge outcropping of rocks on the left side. Once you pass that, there's a clearing and you can stash the truck and the girls can park. He said no one uses this road anymore.'

Kathryn sighed. 'How *does* he know all this? The man absolutely boggles my mind. No wonder he was tops in his field. If you stop to think about it, Alexis, we wouldn't be here doing what we're doing if it wasn't for him.'

Alexis waved her hands in the air. 'He does that click, click, click thing with the maps on the computer. He can bring a dot on a map into full view and you can see the bushes and practically count the blades of grass. Who cares? I see the rocks, Kathryn. There it is, slow down. Turn on your blinker. Jeez, don't miss it. Can you turn this baby in there? Looks kind of narrow to me. Watch it.'

Kathryn rolled her eyes. 'Shut up, Alexis. I can do this.

175

There, see, I did it. The others are following. I wonder if anyone is behind Julia. What if they see all three of us turning in here? For a secluded road, all of a sudden three vehicles turn off. That could arouse some suspicion.'

'I don't think it's secluded. I think it's a bear habitat,' Alexis grinned. 'We aren't going to worry about this, Kathryn.'

Kathryn parked the rig and opened the door. 'No, we're not going to worry about this. Julia, was there much traffic behind you? Did anyone see us turning off here?'

'There was a pickup pretty far back. Why?'

Murphy nudged Kathryn's leg. 'You stay right here with me. Go on, you can lift your leg on that tree. Right back here, Murph. I gotta go myself.'

Alexis pointed. 'I see four thick bushes. Take your pick. Here,' she said, handing her a wad of tissues from her shoulder bag.

'The last time I peed in the bushes I was six years old. My mother told me to pretend I was picking flowers,' Kathryn giggled. 'Alexis said this is bear country so we do it one at a time. Or were you putting me on?'

'I was. Go pee.'

A light rain started to fall just as Alexis said, 'Show time, ladies!'

The women waited until Murphy bounded into the back of the truck before they boosted themselves up and inside. Kathryn lowered the back gate just as Yoko turned on six crank-operated flashlights that Charles had ordered from the Sharper Image catalog. Guaranteed to provide light forever.

Kathryn stood to the side, Murphy next to her as the women stripped off their wigs and shed their clothes. Julia was so pretty in a wholesome way with her thick chestnut hair and light dusting of freckles. In one way she looked plain and in another way she looked elegant. In college she was probably called preppy. When she smiled, which was rare, her whole face lighted up. Kathryn smiled at her assessment of the doctor.

'Julia . . . I . . . want to say something to you. Thank you doesn't seem like enough. We,' she said, waving her hand to indicate the others, 'are just along for the ride in a manner of speaking. It's your knowledge, your expertise, that is accomplishing what we set out to do. When it's your turn, I just want you to know I'll do whatever it takes to do whatever it is you want. That's a given. That's all I wanted to say.'

Julia walked over to Kathryn and hugged her. 'I know that, Kathryn. Now, let's get dressed. I can hardly wait to get on that Night Train again. You know, I just might buy myself one of those when we get back home.'

Alexis dug into her magic sack of disguises. She handed out black push-up bras and skimpy bikinis. 'It's part of a set,' she said. 'One goes with the other. So, you give up your flower underwear for one day, Kathryn, what's the big deal? Leathers for you, Yoko, and you, Julia. Mine are over here. Dolly Parton wigs for everyone. Bandannas for everyone. They'll help secure the wigs because they're heavy. Who wants to be a redhead?'

'Me,' Julia said.

'I want the white one,' Kathryn said.

'The sable brown one is mine,' Yoko said.

'I always wanted to be a blonde,' Alexis giggled. 'A black biker chick with blonde ringlets. Just call me chickee baby.' She pirouetted around the truck in her underwear for the benefit of the others. They clapped and whistled their approval.

Murphy howled when Alexis plopped the blonde wig on her head.

Kathryn, with Julia's help, set up the folding table. Yoko perched on the end to wait for Alexis to open her magic box of cosmetics. 'Mata Hari, I think, Yoko. I'm going to give you a tattoo on the right side of your neck. I have the stuff that will take it off so don't panic. I'm thinking since you're oriental, you might want a small dragon. One that's belching fire.' She wiggled her eyebrows like Groucho Marx. 'You OK with a dragon?'

'Absolutely.'

Alexis's brush flew across Yoko's face. She dipped and swirled, patted and blew on the iridescent powder. 'You want the ring in your nose or your eyebrow?'

'For real?' Yoko said drawing back.

'No. But it will look like it's real. I know what I'm doing.'

'I think I'll take the eyebrow.'

'Done,' Alexis said fastening a small silver hoop to Yoko's thick eyebrows. 'You're starting to look real good, kid,' Alexis said stepping back to view her handiwork. 'Let's plump up those boobs. They're starting to melt. Somebody spit on this decal and paste it on her neck. In the meantime, pick out your own decals. I suggest you put them on the top of your boobs.'

'I don't see anything symbolic,' Kathryn grumbled as she flipped through the artificial tattoos. I want one that says something. I'm going with the teddy bear.'

'I'll take the rose,' Julia said.

'What about you, Alexis?'

'I'm going with Peace and Love,' Alexis said.

'Wow!' Julia and Kathryn said in unison. Yoko shook her rump as she sashayed around the inside of the truck.

They watched as she pulled on her jeans and the leathers. The boots had steel tips with flowers painted on the sides. The vest with the silver knobs was the last thing she put on. Her breasts spilled out the top, her cleavage deep and seductive. The dragon wiggled on her neck each time she took a deep breath.

Julia slid on to the table. 'Alexis, you might want to put on a pair of latex gloves,' she said quietly.

Alexis bent over until she was eye level with Julia. 'I'm not afraid of you, Julia. I don't need the gloves. We aren't exactly exchanging body fluids here. Now, sit still so I can make you more beautiful than you already are.' She waited while Julia knuckled her eyes. 'OK, now, I'm going to make you look like Anna Nicole Smith, that blonde bimbo who married that really rich old man.'

She was as good as her word. Fifteen minutes later, Julia slid off the table. 'Ta da!' she said jiggling to unheard runway music.

'Fantastic!' Kathryn giggled.

'OK, Barbarella, you're next.'

Kathryn hopped up on the table. 'Do it!' she said dramatically.

Alexis's brush swirled and dipped again, up and down, across and then back up. In the blink of an eye, Kathryn sported outrageous false eyelashes that were curly enough to hold a pencil. 'This is the most petulant mouth I've ever seen in my life,' she said staring into the mirror Alexis held up. 'I love it! I didn't think it was possible to look this *slutty*.'

'We look like tramps,' Yoko said peering at Julia.

'Yoo hoo!' Alexis said. They turned around and gasped in awe. Who was this long-legged creature in the leopard skin jumpsuit that was unzipped to the waist?

'Holy shit!' Kathryn said.

'Holy shit is right,' Julia said.

Yoko was totally speechless as Alexis fastened her leathers and then slipped into the black leather vest. Her boots were covered in leopard skin and had three-inch heels. She looked to be six feet tall. Murphy growled as he sniffed her feet.

'What time is it?' Julia asked.

'Ten minutes of eight,' Kathryn said staring down at her watch. 'Yeah, yeah, it's time to roll out our transportation. I didn't see any road lights so that means it's gonna be dark. Just stay behind me once we get to the main road. We don't have far to go so nothing should go awry. Oh, shit, it's pouring rain.'

Alexis dived into her sack of goodies and came up with four black ponchos. Don't thank me, thank Charles,' she said tossing one to each of them.

Kathryn pulled hers on. 'Come on Murphy, time to settle you down for the night.'

Inside the cab, Kathryn shooed Murphy to the back where a bed was set up. 'Here's your baby,' she said handing the dog a battered, bald Raggedy Ann doll. 'Here's a new, fresh chewie and your ball. Your treat is by the water bowl. Your food is in your dish. You guard this truck with your life. We'll be back in a little while. I know you understand everything I'm saying, Murph. This is important. Don't bark.'

The big dog licked her hand before he stretched out on the single mattress.

'Did you guys lock the cars? Of course you did. Just let me lock up here and we can be on our way. Why the hell did it have to rain? We're going to be leaving tire marks all over the damn place,' Kathryn muttered as she straddled the '67 Electra Glide. She pressed the button and the machine came to life. She felt Yoko settle herself behind her just as Alexis's '93 Softail's engine turned over. She waited a moment for the sound of the FXSTB Night Train to come alive.

The night was pitch-black as Kathryn led the group out to the main road. She looked both ways before she peeled out on to the macadam, Alexis and Julia behind her. She could feel Yoko's death grip around her waist. Hysteria bubbled up to her throat. We must look like something out of a scary Halloween movie, she thought as she crawled along the highway.

The minute she saw the blaze of neon lighting ahead she felt all the tenseness leave her body. She swerved into the parking lot of the Lone Pine Retreat, tooled around to the back and cut the engine. The others parked next to her.

'The temperature's dropping,' Julia said.

'Is that important?' Alexis asked anxiously.

'No. I was just making conversation.'

'Listen up, we wear these ponchos till we get inside. We hang them up and then we *strut*, ladies, to the bar. Strut. We do not sashay, we do not slink, we do not walk, we strut. No fancy drinks. Hard liquor. Scotch. That's what biker chicks drink. I read that in one of Charles's magazines. We are on the prowl, so look obvious. We're easy but make them work for it. You ready?'

Three ponchos bobbed up and down as the quartet ran for the main entrance.

It was like a million other bars: steamy, smoky and sleazy. It was just one big room with tables positioned around the bar. They were greeted with whistles, hoots and explicit suggestions. They waved and smiled as they swung their legs over the bar stool.

'What's your pleasure, ladies?' the bartender leered.

'Scotch on the rocks. A double,' Kathryn said.

'I'll have the same,' Alexis said.

'Make that three,' Julia said.

'Four,' Yoko squeaked.

Kathryn had to stand up to fish in her jeans pocket for money. She half turned so that the group at the long table could get a better view of her right breast and the tattoo. She slapped a fifty dollar bill down on the bar.

Julia reached for her drink and downed it in two swallows. She thumped the glass down on the bar and swivelled around, her long legs stretched out in front of her. She looked pointedly at the men sitting at the table. 'That's some impressive machinery out front. We're on our way to the Harley Davidson show. Would any of you be interested in buying an FXSTB Night Train? Sugar here is selling her '93 Softail, too.'

'I might be interested in the Night Train,' Charles said getting up from the table and walking over to the bar. 'Is it outside?'

'Sure is, honey. Be glad to show it to you after we get something to eat. We've been riding all day.'

'Why don't you ladies join us. I placed our order but I don't see a problem adding four more steaks to the order. Hey guys, swing four more chairs over here.'

'Well sure, we'd love to join you. We got nothing better to do and we want to wait out the rain. Y'all staying around here or what?'

'We're camping in the Alabama Hills,' Charles said.

'You guys on a run?' Alexis asked.

'Yeah,' someone shouted from the far end of the table.

'We did it for victims of violent crimes,' someone else shouted. 'You *ladies* want to kick in some bucks?'

'Sure,' they said in unison as each one of them handed over a hundred dollar bill.

The men sat up a little straighter when Charles scooped up the money and thanked them.

'So, where are y'all from?' Kathryn drawled.

'LA,' someone said. 'How about you?'

'Oregon,' Yoko said.

'So, what do y'all do, do y'all work or do you just . . . ride around?' Kathryn asked as she maneuvered herself to the far end of the table to get as far away from Wagstaff as she could.

'Both,' Dr Clark Wagstaff said.

Julia sat down next to him. 'So, what do you do?' she purred. 'Claudia Abbott,' she said holding out her hand.

'Clark Wagstaff.' He pumped her hand for a full thirty seconds. 'I'm an oral surgeon. How about you?' Wagstaff asked as he eyed the tattoo on top of her left breast.

'I paint murals inside churches,' Julia said. 'The bikes are just a weekend hobby.'

'What about your friends? By the way, I might be interested in the Night Train. I'd like to take a look at it later.'

'Well, sure, that's OK by me. Goes to the highest bidder. Candy down there at the end of the table makes muffins. Best muffins in the state of Oregon. Stella, over there, has her own bike shop in Portland. Makes money hand over fist. Mei Ling is a massage therapist. When she walks on your back you'd swear you died and went to heaven. She knows *exactly* how to please a man. So, what's good to eat in this dump? This is a dump, you know. Excuse me, I want to talk to that gentleman over there about my Night Train.'

Julia wiggled her way over to where Charles was

sitting. He looked at her with open admiration. 'It's hard to believe you ride a Night Train,' he said.

'You wouldn't believe the teacher I had. How's it going?' she asked under her breath.

'Another hour and they'll all be rolling on the floor. They're all heavy drinkers except our two. They pretty much have their wits about them,' Charles said sotto voce.

'The food should be coming out any minute now.'

'I didn't order yet,' Julia said.

'I took the liberty of ordering ahead of time. Steaks, baked potatoes and salad.

'I'd like to make a toast to all of you for taking the time to make this run for such a worthy cause. Bottoms up, gentlemen,' he said. 'To charity and the fine people who donate unselfishly of their time and money.'

'Hear! Hear!' the men shouted raucously.

'And now for the winner of the restored, one-of-a-kind Indian. Did you all put your names in this shoebox?' Charles asked pointing to the middle of the table. Heads bobbed up and down. 'Good. Why don't we have one of these little ladies pick the winning name?' Charles pointed to Alexis who stood up and leaned over the table. The two men across from her gasped when she daintily held up the little square of paper.

'Bobby Tufts, you are the winner of the Indian! This calls for a toast! To Bobby Tufts, may he ride in glory on his new Indian!'

'Man, did I really win? Me! Did you hear that, guys? I never won anything in my life. Man, this is so great. Wait till my wife hears about this. A toast, guys! To this kind, generous man. What's your name again?' he asked drunkenly.

'Alistair Fitzsimmions,' Charles said regally. 'You're right, this is one of those bottoms up toasts. To Bobby Tufts!'

'Now, Mr Tufts, where do you want the bike shipped?'

Bobby Tufts pulled a card out of his shirt pocket and handed it over. 'My home address is on the bottom of the card.'

'I see you're a loan officer at the Wells Fargo bank. Now I know where to go if I want a loan.' Tufts doubled over laughing.

The food arrived, thick T-Bone steaks, fat, loaded potatoes and a delicious looking garden salad.

Two hours went by before Julia stood up and said, 'I'm going to see if it's still raining. I think it's time for us to move on. Thanks for the dinner and drinks, Mr Fitzsimmions. Do you want to look at the bike now or did you change your mind? Dr Wagstaff over there said he wanted to look at it, too.'

Alexis stood up and flexed her shoulders. 'Hey, you guys, are any of you going to the Testicle Festival in Montana this year? If so, we'll see you there!' she said brightly.

'Yeah, yeah, we're all going,' Bobby Tufts said.

'See ya. Nice meeting all of you,' Kathryn said.

'Hey, Sam, come take a look at this lady's bike,' Wagstaff said to Sam La Fond who was staggering to his feet.

Kathryn and Alexis both grabbed three full bottles of beer off the table as they followed Julia and Yoko outside. Kathryn shoved her bottles into Yoko's hands so she could unscrew the bottle of Rohypnol that was in her pocket. In the darkness with the rain pelting them, she had no idea how much went into the beer bottles.

'That's a beauty, all right. Bet you want a pretty penny for it, eh?'

'A lot of pretty pennies. We're staying at the inn tonight but plan to leave around seven. We're heading north. If you want to come by early and take a look at it in the daylight, feel free. What about you, Dr Wagstaff?' Julia said holding out a bottle of beer to him. He gulped at it. Yoko held out a second bottle to Sam La Fond. Charles pretended to drink from his.

'Where's the car we're supposed to transport them in?' Kathryn hissed.

'The Ford Mustang parked next to the pickup truck. The key is in the ignition,' Charles whispered back. 'I'll be by in the morning. I have to see about getting my guests back safe and sound to the camp ground now. I'm very interested,' he said loudly for the benefit of the others.

'I'm not interested,' Wagstaff said slipping to the ground.

'I think your friend is drunk,' Alexis said. 'Aren't you going to pick him up?'

'Why should I?' La Fond asked belligerently.

'It's raining. He could drown.'

'What's it to you?'

'Absolutely nothing,' Yoko said. 'Just out of curiosity, Mr La Fond, how many women did you and your buddy rape on these rides.'

'Lots and lots and lots,' he mumbled as he fell on top of his friend.

'I told you, Kathryn,' Yoko said gently. 'Hurry, we have to get them in the car before someone comes out.

'He won't remember the question when he wakes up, Kathryn,' Julia said just as gently.

It was better than a precision drill as the four women

grabbed Wagstaff's legs and arms and dumped him unceremoniously on to the back seat. They did the same thing with La Fond. When he rolled on to the floor, Yoko shrugged. 'Oh well.'

'Looks like we're set to go. Yoko, wait till we pull out and you stay on our trail. Let's go,' Kathryn said straddling the cycle. She peeled out on to the road, the others right behind her.

Kathryn slowed to a bare crawl when she noticed oncoming headlights. She didn't pick up speed until the lights were out of sight. She swerved on to the rough road and tore down it at full throttle, the rain pouring down her back. She was soaked to the skin when she opened the tailgate to yank down the ramp. She was back on the Electra Glide and roaring up the plank a minute later, Alexis and Julia right behind her.

'Leave the headlights on, Yoko, until we get them inside. Same deal, sisters, feet and arms. No need to be gentle,' Kathryn said.

'Listen, I have to take Murphy out. I'll be with you in a minute.'

Yoko held out a napkin wrapped package. 'Take your time,' Yoko said. 'I gathered up some of the steak bones for Murphy to chew on. Do you wish to give it to him? There's quite a bit of meat on them. Those men did not eat much. It was such a waste of food. I remember the days when I had only scraps to eat.'

'That was sweet of you, Yoko. Thanks. Hopefully, it will keep him occupied. He's going to know there are strangers in the back. I don't know how he'll react. He might bark his head off and there's no way I can control that.'

'So what. Dogs bark all the time. This,' Yoko said

waving her arms at the trees, 'is pretty far out. We are soaked, Kathryn. We need to get out of our wet clothes.'

Kathryn unlocked the cab and climbed up. Murphy licked her face and then snatched the napkin wrapped bundle out of her hands. 'Yoko, thanks for . . . You know.'

'Yes, I know. You are welcome, Kathryn.'

Fifteen minutes later, both men were inside the truck and the tailgate was closed and locked down. 'First things first,' Julia said. 'We need to get out of these wet clothes and into dry ones. Stand still for a moment while I look around. The sheets are in place, the entire floor is covered. That's good. The table is up, there's a clean sheet on it. We have a dozen towels. The lights are on. That's good. I can see perfectly. Gloves everyone. Who goes first?' she asked tying her surgical mask behind her head.

The women looked at one another. 'La Fond didn't drink as much of the beer as Wagstaff did,' Alexis volunteered. 'You better do him first. Put a drop on his tongue just to be sure.'

Julia held up her gloved hands. 'It's up to you three to boost him up to the table. Yoko, take both his feet, Kathryn and Alexis, grab him under his arms. There you go. Take off his pants. On second thought, just pull them down.' She picked up the scalpel. She looked up over the mask. 'Hospital procedure or quick and dirty?'

'Just do the Q and D,' Alexis said.

Kathryn leaned against the wall of the truck, her eyes on Julia's hands. How deft and sure she was. She said it wasn't brain surgery, still, without her skill, this wouldn't be happening. She blinked. It was happening. She was seeing it with her own eyes. She almost jumped out of her skin when she heard La Fond's jewels drop into a small pickle jar. Even from this distance she could read the Mt. Olive label. Two down and one to go.

'That's a very nice, neat bandage. Will it come loose?' Yoko queried.

'Probably. When they start rummaging for the missing goods, they could dislodge it. Depends on how frantic they get. OK, this guy's done! Next!'

While the women lifted La Fond off the table, Julia stripped off her gloves and pulled on two new pairs. She waited, her hands in the air until Wagstaff was on the table. Yoko yanked at his pants until she had them down around his ankles.

Kathryn sucked in her breath when Julia picked up the scalpel. Ten minutes later, Wagstaff's nuts plunked into a mayonnaise jar. She slid to the floor of the truck and put her head between her knees.

'What are we supposed to do now? My brain's frozen. I can't think. What?' Kathryn shouted. 'Somebody tell me.'

'Hey, take it easy, Kathryn. We're taking them in the two cars back to their camp ground. We put them in their tents and split. Charles will be there to point out which tents belong to them. It's OK that you forgot. We have it under control. Now, let's move. If we fold up the legs of the table and lower it to the floor, we can slide it down the ramp and we won't have to carry them so far. We can drive the cars right up to the opening,' Alexis said.

Kathryn shook her head to clear it. 'Has Murphy been barking all this time?'

'Yes,' Yoko said.

'Julia and I are driving. C'mon, Kathryn, look alive here.'

'I'm alive. Let's do it.'

Charles waved the light from a small flash light to show them he was waiting. They drove the cars as far as they could before they climbed out. It took fifteen minutes before the men were settled in their sleeping bags. Yoko bent over and zipped them up. She smiled at Kathryn.

'Get out of here, now,' Charles said.

'What about the Mustang?' Julia asked.

'I'll drive it deep into the bushes. Did you wipe it clean?'

'I did,' Yoko said.

'We're outta here,' Alexis said climbing into the driver's seat of the car.

'Wait a minute,' Kathryn said. She unzipped the flap of the tent and stuck her head in. 'In the words of President Bill Clinton, gentlemen, "I feeeel your painnnn".'

Charles clapped his hand over his mouth to keep from laughing as Kathryn sprinted for the car.

Back at their home base, Kathryn yanked at the tailgate. 'Clean up time! Somebody is watching over us. All this rain has to do is keep up for another couple of hours, and it looks like it will, and our tracks will be washed away.'

They did what they had to do. The motorcycles were stashed in the back, the wheels on the tarp Kathryn had spread earlier. The sheets, towels, bloody gauze pads and gloves were shoved into heavy-duty trash bags. The table would be dumped as soon as they found a suitable trash container, the trash bag somewhere in San Francisco. The mayonnaise and pickles were placed with the Snapple bottle in the lunch box. Kathryn handed it to Julia.

The women stood outside the truck, the rain beating down on them. Their arms stretched out till they formed a tight little circle. No one said a word.

Kathryn climbed into the truck. She waved. 'I'll see you all in five days.'

The CB was in Kathryn's hand the minute she crossed the state line into Kansas.

'This is Big Sis. You there, Bugle Beagle?'

'I'm here, Sis. Where you been? Had a call out to you.'

'I know, Bugle, but stuff started caving in on me and I had to split for a while. Went off to Bermuda for some down time. What's up, Bugle? The messages sounded urgent.'

A bird swooped down and flew across the windshield. Murphy let out an ear-splitting bark and lunged at the window. 'Shhh, boy, it was just a bird. Sorry, Bugle.'

'The guy said he was a District Attorney in the District. You know my feelings on the law and how they hound you guys. Said it was important and you should call right away. I didn't tell him squat. You better give him a call. What'd you do with the dog when you went to Bermuda?'

Dog. Oh shit. Screwup number five or was it six? Bile rose up to her throat. 'I left him with a friend in San Francisco. Why?'

'No reason. I like dogs. You said he was the best thing that happened to you after Al died. Listen, drive with the angels and I'll keep in touch. You carrying lettuce or squash?'

'Romaine lettuce. I got two extra boxes if you want some.'

'Nah. I hate rabbit food. I'm a steak and potatoes man. Take care, Sis.'

'You, too, Bugle. Over and out.'

She reached over behind Murphy and dialed Myra's number on the special cell phone. 'Hi,' she said in a shaky voice. 'I just crossed the line into Kansas and called the dispatcher in Roanoke because the DA back there has been trying to get in touch with me. We had a nice talk. He wanted to know what I did with Murphy when I went to Bermuda. Imagine that.'

'Why don't I put Charles on the phone, Kathryn?'

'That sounds good.'

'Kathryn, it's so nice to talk to you again. Mike Daniels drove from Sacramento to San Francisco to pick up your dog. He lives at 3055 5th Avenue in Sacramento. He dropped him off at the airport when you landed.'

'Thanks. See you in a few days.' Kathryn clicked off the power and then clicked it back on. She dialed the number Jack Emery had given Bugle. She punched in the extension and waited.

'Jack Emery here.'

'Mr Emery, this is Kathryn Lucas. I understand you've been trying to reach me. I just got your message.'

'You just got it! I thought you truckers lived on your CBs.'

Kathryn took a deep breath and let it out slowly. 'Some do, some don't. I don't. The reason I just got your message was I just returned from Bermuda. I needed some time to . . . think. I know you had no way of knowing this but my husband just passed away recently. I needed to get away. What is it you want from me, Mr Emery?'

'Did you make a delivery to Myra Rutledge and did you stay overnight and sleep in your truck while it was parked at her estate?'

'Why are you asking me these questions? Technically you're the police. I didn't do anything wrong.

Hell, the woman hasn't even paid for the stuff I dropped off.'

'What did you drop off?'

'First, I think you better tell me why you want to know.'

'I'm the one asking the questions, Ms Lucas.'

'And I'm the one that isn't answering. If there's nothing else, Mr Emery, I'm going to hang up. I need to pay attention to the road. By the way, I'm in Kansas.'

'When do you expect to hit Virginia?'

'Three days, four at the most. I have to drop off some lettuce in North Carolina.'

'I'd like you to stop by my offices when you get here.'

'Again, Mr Emery, why? Look, if those bathroom fixtures are defective it has nothing to do with me. I just pick up and deliver. You're making this sound like I need a lawyer. If I do, I'll give you her name now and you can take this all up with her. I might be picking up a load of pine straw in North Carolina so I can't say for sure where I'll be. She'll know how to get in touch with me.'

'OK, what's her name? You did say her, didn't you?'

'Nicole Quinn. Her office is on G Street. If there's nothing else, I have to sign off here.' Kathryn allowed a smile to tug at the corners of her mouth when she heard him curse under his breath. She broke the connection and tossed the cell phone on the seat next to Murphy. He nudged it until it was behind him. He stretched out, his tennis ball between his paws.

Kathryn yanked at the baseball cap that said Lucas Trucking, settling it more firmly on her head. She adjusted her sunglasses and concentrated on the road in front of her as she tried to imagine what Clark Wagstaff, Sam La

Fond and Sid Lee were doing. Murphy slept on the seat next to her.

Jack Emery stared at the phone on his desk. His heart pounded in his chest when he bellowed for his assistant. 'Harry, get on the horn with Judge Olsen. I want a court order to impound Kathryn Lucas's truck. The minute she crosses the state line into Virginia, I want that truck snatched. I don't give a shit what's inside it. And while you're at it, put out an all points on her. Pick it up yourself and get it to me as soon as you can. Why are you still sitting there? When I tell you to move your ass, I mean move your ass. Now, goddamn it!'

Jack leaned back in his chair staring at nothing, his eyes glazed. A sick feeling settled in the pit of his stomach. He reached for the phone and managed to send the papers on his desk flying in all directions. He bent down to pick them up. He stacked them any old way on his desk and then blinked at what he was seeing.

'Hey, Conrad, come here a minute,' he called to another ADA. 'Does the name Isabelle Flanders ring a bell with you? I know I heard that name somewhere. Take a look at this picture. It's kind of grainy because it's a fax. Does she look familiar to you?'

'Yeah. Yeah, she made the news a few years back when she killed a whole family driving in a hurry somewhere. Your girlfriend defended her. Lost the case. I think she was an architect. Why?'

'Just a detail that has to do with something I'm working on,' Jack responded, sticking to his credo of not divulging details with those around him. It wasn't that he tried to hog the glory like Nik always accused him of doing, he was simply thorough, preferring to stack his bricks in a neat column so they wouldn't tumble down and make him look like a fool.

The sick feeling was getting worse. He reached for the phone and for a second time, ignored it. 'Conrad, call Judge Olsen's office and tell him I need another court order for Myra Rutledge's house. Get Harry on the phone and tell him not to come back here unless he has both of them in his hands.'

'Why am I doing your shit work, Emery?'

'Because I told you to do it and I have seniority. Just fucking do it, Conrad.'

This time when he reached for the phone, he actually dialed the number he wanted. Nik's cell phone number.

'Nik, it's Jack,' he said the minute Nikki said hello. 'Listen to me, Nik. I'm on my way out to the farm. I have a court order so don't try to evade me. We need to talk. I have the court order,' he lied, 'but I don't want to come out there as Jack Emery DA, I want to come out and talk to you as Jack Emery, your friend. We were friends, Nik. I'll be there in an hour and a half.'

'All right, Jack.'

Jack beelined for the men's room where he lost his lunch.

Twelve

Charles and Myra watched as Nikki walked out to the long driveway. By craning their necks they could see Jack Emery's car at the gate. Myra reached for Charles's hand. 'This isn't good, is it, dear?'

'No, it isn't good. The really bizarre part of Mr Emery's case is Kathryn really didn't have anything to do with spiriting Marie and her family to safety. I just don't know at the moment how it is all going to play out. It looks to me like he's studying the High Voltage sign attached to the gate. I'm sure he's wondering if it's real or not.'

Myra leaned over and pressed her face against the window. 'I think he is studying it, Charles. I think it was a stroke of genius to screw that sign on the gate. It gives one pause for thought. Are we, you know, going to . . . *take him out*?' Myra asked nervously. 'That could stir up a whole can of worms, Charles.'

'I know. I'm thinking, Myra. I wish I knew what they were saying to each other.'

'Let's make a cake, Charles,' Myra said pulling him away from the window. 'One of those seven layer chocolate ones with pudding between the layers and real thick frosting all around. Nikki's going to need something sweet after this little talk she's having with Jack. She loves him so much. Love can be blind at times. I'll turn on the oven.'

Outside their line of vision, Nikki walked up to what Myra called the walk-through gate and out to Jack's car. She opened the door and climbed in. She sighed wishing she could lean over and kiss him. She realized she could if she wanted to. Instead she said, 'I really don't want to love you anymore, Jack. However, I think I'm one of those people who only love once. Don't look at me like that, Jack.'

Jack pointed to the High Voltage sign. 'Isn't that new? Why does Myra Rutledge need a sign like that?' Nikki shrugged. 'Listen, Nik, I need to talk to you. Jack and Nik, OK? Not prosecutor and lawyer. Can we do that?'

'We can try, Jack.' She shivered inside her light sweater. Jack pulled her closer and put his arm around her shoulders. She knew she should move away but she didn't because his arms felt so good. A flood of memories washed through her.

'This is what I have, Nik. I'm going to lay it all out for you. There's a strange group of women who come out here. You defended Isabelle Flanders and lost her case. Nobody could have won that one so you shouldn't condemn yourself. Then there's the doctor married to the senator. Very high profile couple. She's not operating anymore for some strange reason. Tops in her field, too. Guess she's going to fill up her days by playing cards with Myra. The Chinese girl and the tall, leggy black girl just don't fit the scene. Do you know what I mean? They're more your age and yet they come out here to do whatever it is they do. And Myra couldn't seem to get her card games straight.'

Nikki forced a laugh. 'Sometimes they play Fish. It's

more the companionship than the card playing. Myra needs to be around younger people. Are you saying you think all these women helped me spirit Marie Lewellen away? That is so outrageous, so off the top, I can't even give it credence. I had nothing to do with it, Jack. I swear to you on Barbara. What's it going to take to convince you?'

'I don't know. My gut is telling me I have to pay attention. I'm trying to do that. I want to see all the stuff Lucas delivered. She said she slept in the truck the night of the storm. I have some trouble with that. Why didn't Myra invite her to stay in the house? That would have been the decent thing to do. She lied to me about the driver, too. She referred to the driver as him. Not her. Him. She was very specific about him and his dog.'

'I can't answer that, Jack. I wasn't here when she talked to you. I knew the driver was a woman because Myra said it was a woman. I remember thinking she must be pretty strong to drive a big rig like that.' She shrugged. 'A slip of the tongue. Whatever. Myra thinks women should stay home and knit and do good deeds. That's fine if you don't have to work for a living. Obviously the driver has to work for a living in order to eat and pay her bills.'

Jack stared off into space. 'I have an all points out on her and the truck. The minute she crosses the state line we're hauling her in. We'll impound the truck and sweep it clean.'

Nikki shrugged again. 'I guess you have to do what you have to do. It's not going to get you anywhere, Jack, because she had nothing to do with it. You're grasping at straws here to make yourself look good.'

'Is that what you *really* think, Nik? It happened on my watch. My boss is on my ass. You're threatening to sue the department. You know for every action there is a reaction. You're the one who told me that.'

'I'll represent Ms Lucas if you kick up a fuss, Jack. All this ugly stuff will come out. That probable cause crap isn't going to hold up and you know it. Myra is *very* influential. She knows everyone worth knowing. Senator Webster will come down on you like a ton of bricks if you even mention his wife and Myra in the same breath. She lost a million dollars, Jack. Yeah, I know you think she has money to burn but she doesn't. She donates to every worthy cause there is. She'll hire some thousand-buck-an-hour attorney and he'll smash you to a pulp before you can say, I'll see you in court.'

'Is that supposed to scare me, Nik?'

'No, of course not. I'm just telling you what you're up against if you take on Myra. That's your plan, isn't it? I know the way you operate, Jack. You're working this on your own because, as you said, you like to get everything airtight before you spring your trap. You really should share all this with your boss before you end up making a mess of things. Keep your friends close, your enemies even closer. That kind of thing, right?'

Jack's stomach worked itself into a knot. 'Let's check out those bathroom fixtures.'

'Why not,' Nikki said getting out of the car. 'Be sure to bring that court order. Myra will want to see it.'

Jack plucked it off the dashboard and handed it to Nikki. 'OK, this says you can search the garage, the barn and the house. Let's go. Oh, one more thing, when you haul the truck driver in, I want to be there. I'll do it pro bono. I mean it, Jack, don't question her until and unless I'm present.'

Jack snorted. 'How do you even know she'll want you

to represent her? If she has nothing to hide why does she need a lawyer?'

'To protect her from you. Besides, I am her attorney. She came to see me once but I couldn't help her.'

'What did she want you to do for her?'

Nikki swatted him with the court order. 'That's client–attorney privilege. You know better than to even ask. Go ahead, I'll wait here. The stuff is in the garage. There's a crowbar in there if you want to open the boxes.'

When Jack joined her twenty minutes later she said, 'Four bathtubs, one misty green, one powder blue, garden tub in daffodil yellow and one in shell pink. Matching shower enclosures. Toilets same color with matching toilet seats. Two double sinks, one single and one with three basins. The vanities have to be built. Did I forget anything?'

'Yeah, the blueprints.'

'Myra can show you those. I wish you'd stop being such an asshole.'

Jack stomped ahead of her. 'Let's go see those blue-prints. Of all the architects in town and the surrounding area, why did Myra pick Flanders? She has a shitty reputation.'

'You'll have to ask Myra yourself, Jack. Bathroom remodeling is not my forte. Aren't you going to check the barn?'

'When I'm ready,' Jack snapped. Nikki opened the screen door that squeaked just the way a screen door is supposed to squeak.

'Oooh, what smells so good? Are you making a choc-olate cake, Myra?'

'Yes, dear. Just for you. Hello, Jack, how are you?' Myra asked coolly.

'Fine, thank you.' He nodded in Charles's direction. 'I'd like to see the blueprints for the bathrooms.' His tone was just as cool as Myra's.

'Charles, take Jack to the summer pantry. Isabelle is working there because I didn't have any other available space for her. Do not *touch* anything.

'Would you rather have stuffed peppers or pork chops for dinner, dear?'

'Stuffed peppers. How about pickled red beets and the wilted lettuce with lots of bacon in it. Lots and lots of mashed potatoes.'

'I think Charles can manage that. I wish I was half the cook he is.'

'Satisfied?' Nikki asked sourly when Jack followed Charles into the kitchen. 'Now what? If you want to check the rest of the house, go to it. He has a court order, Myra. That means he can do whatever he damn pleases. That includes going through your drawers.'

'*I don't think so!*' Myra said rearing up on her chair. 'You try doing that, young man, and I'll call the police commissioner personally. And the mayor.'

Jack wagged his finger under Nikki's nose. 'You really are a troublemaker. I'm not going through your drawers, Myra. However, I will open your closets and look inside. Don't worry, I won't *touch* anything.'

'Don't expect us to help you. Go to it, Sherlock,' Nikki said.

Jack returned to the kitchen thirty minutes late, his face bleak with disappointment.

'I guess I'll see you to the gate. Ooops, you gotta do the barn, don't you?'

'Yes, I have to do the barn,' Jack said slamming his way through the open doorway. Nikki followed him.

'Don't spook the horses and don't—'

'*Touch* anything.' Jack whirled around, his face full of disgust and anger. 'What is it with you rich people?' He looked down at his hands. 'Do you think us poor commoners have some kind of disease on our hands? That we aren't good enough to touch your precious belongings? I'm doing my goddamn job is what I'm doing. If you don't like it, screw you.'

'Jack, I didn't mean . . . Jack . . .?'

When he returned, his face was still full of disgust. 'You better walk me to the gate and let me out so I don't *touch* anything. Right now I'm wondering how the hell I ever fell in love with you.'

'Jack . . .'

'Get out of my way, Nik. Don't worry, I'll have someone call you when we bring Kathryn Lucas in for questioning.'

'I'm . . . sorry, Jack.'

'Sorry is just a word. Now get the hell out of my way.'

Tears streaming down her cheeks, Nikki turned away.

Fifty-six hours later, Kathryn saw and heard the siren at the same moment the Malinois slammed his body against the door. 'Easy, Murph, easy. I see them.' She slowed the rig and pulled to the shoulder a quarter of a mile down the road. In the side view mirror she saw the cop exit his squad car. She watched as he leaned against the door. A second police car came out of nowhere and pulled in front of her. The second cop got out of his car and started to walk toward her just as the first cop swung around to the passenger side of the rig. Murphy, his hair on end, lunged at the door.

The CB squawked. 'Hey, out there, this is Cornball, looks like Big Sis hit a spot of trouble. Sis, need any help?'

Kathryn picked up the CB. 'Don't know yet, Cornball. Stay on my six and let's play it out. I'm riding empty this leg and heading home.'

'Gotcha, Sis. Blue Rider is a quarter of a mile up and slowing down. Give us two blasts and we'll close in.'

'You got it, Cornball. I'll leave the power on so you can hear.' She leaned out the window but didn't say anything. Murphy was in her lap, his head next to hers.

'Are you Kathryn Lucas?'

'I am.'

'We're impounding this truck. Follow the first car. I'll be behind you.'

'Do you have a warrant?'

'No, ma'am, but there is one at headquarters. The District Attorney said you would come in willingly.'

'All right but only if my lawyer is present. If you can't arrange that, I'm not moving this truck. Call it in and let me know the answer.' Kathryn moved back from the window. Murphy continued to growl at the officer standing below him.

Kathryn risked a glance in the rear-view mirror. Her eyebrows shot upward. She started to laugh when she saw the caravan of eighteen-wheelers spread out across the road. She looked ahead and saw the same bridge a tenth of a mile up the road.

Ah, the power of the open road. Alan always said trucking was a noble profession because on any given day the drivers could bring the entire country to its knees simply by not turning on the engines. For one brief moment she felt almost invincible.

His hand on his holster, the first cop bellowed, 'What the hell is going on here?' His voice sounded jittery to Kathryn's ears. She smiled.

The second cop looked back over his shoulder and then forward. Kathryn could see the sweat bead up on his forehead. The first cop looked up at Kathryn and said, 'Get on that CB of yours and tell those truckers to disperse now.'

Kathryn picked up the CB and said, 'This is Big Sis. Listen up. These two fine officers standing next to my truck told me to get on this CB and tell you to *disssssperse* now. She listened, the grin staying on her face as the truckers, one by one, professed to have serious engine problems.

'Officer, they seem to be having difficulty with their engines.'

'Tell them to call the goddamn auto club!'

'This is Big Sis again, boys. These fine officers want you to call the auto club.' She listened, her face going pink.

She leaned out the window. 'I don't think you want to know what they said, but they also want to know if you have the number of the auto club. So, is my lawyer going to be there or not?'

'Yeah.'

'Then why didn't you say so?' She reached for the CB. 'Cornball, this is Big Sis. I'm OK. I'm going to follow the cops. They're impounding my truck and taking me to the District Attorney's office. I'm going willingly. That's just for the record, OK. Thanks for your help.'

'Anytime, Sis.'

As each truck roared past her, it gave two sharp blasts

that she returned in kind. Murphy howled his outrage at these goings on.

'I know exactly what you did so don't try it again,' the first cop said.

'Officer,' Kathryn said sweetly, 'those truckers would have sat there indefinitely. Even the National Guard couldn't have *disssspersed* them.'

'Oh yeah,' the first cop blustered.

'Yeah,' Kathryn shot back.

They sat opposite one another, glaring. Nikki felt the urge to cry just the way she'd cried when Jack was at the farm. The phone rang.

'Emery here,' Jack growled. 'OK.' He looked away and said, 'They're bringing her up now.'

Nikki remained silent, her face miserable.

Jack eyed the Belgian Malinois standing at Kathryn's side. 'Have a seat. This won't take long. Your attorney has given us forty-five minutes to sweep your truck and then you can pick it up. I want a sworn statement from you and then you're free to go.'

Kathryn looked at Nikki who nodded.

'Before you ask me anything, Mr Emery, I want it on the record that I'm willing to take a lie detector test. Any time, any place.'

'Write that down, Jack,' Nikki said coolly.

'I wrote it down. If I think it's necessary, I'll notify you.'

'In writing,' Nikki said.

Jack lowered his head. 'Do you know Marie Lewellen or any member of her family?'

'No.'

'Were you ever introduced to her or to any member

of her family? Did you ever see Marie Lewellen and her family?'

'No and no.'

'Did you, on the night of January 21, take Marie Lewellen and her family somewhere in your truck?'

'No.'

'Did anyone other than yourself drive your truck on the night of January 21?'

'No.'

'Why were you at Myra Rutledge's estate on the night of January 21?'

'I delivered bathroom fixtures. The storm got worse as I was unloading and I was tired. I asked Mrs Rutledge if it was OK to sleep in my truck on the property and she said yes. She said I could sleep in the house, but I had the dog and I knew he wouldn't be comfortable in a strange place.'

'Were there other cars there when you arrived?'

'I don't know. It was already dark. I didn't pay attention.'

'When you left the next day were there cars there?'

'Yes.'

'One last question. Do you know where Marie Lewellen and her family are? Did you, perhaps, overhear people discussing her disappearance or hear other people say where she might be?'

'No to both your questions.'

'Is that your sworn statement, then?'

'Yes, that's my sworn statement.'

Jack pressed the print button and waited for the form to slide out of the printer. 'Read through it, let your attorney see it and if everything is in order, sign your name at the bottom.'

Kathryn read through her statement and handed it to Nikki who read it thoroughly. 'It's OK to sign it, Kathryn.'

'Can I go?'

'That was some stunt you pulled out there on the interstate,' Jack said coolly, his eyes on Nikki.

Kathryn remained silent.

'What stunt?' Nikki asked.

'Her trucker friends blocked the interstate. They sandwiched the two police officers into a square. Said they had engine trouble.'

'Anything's possible,' Nikki said. 'How much longer, Jack?'

Jack looked at his watch. 'They should be finishing up right now. As soon as the sweep team calls and tells me everything is OK, you're free to go. Until that call comes in, you stay right here.'

The call came in five minutes later. Both women watched Jack as he listened to the voice on the other end of the phone. He hung up and threw his pencil across the room. 'They said,' he enunciated each word carefully, 'the truck was clean as a whistle.'

'I always vacuum it out after a run. I just dropped off a load of pine straw in North Carolina. No one wants to have you haul a load of produce in a dirty truck. In addition to that, I'm a neat, tidy person. Make whatever you want out of that, Mr Emery. Is this the end of it?'

'It's the end of it, isn't it, Jack?' Nikki said coldly.

'For now,' Jack said.

'Let's get some lunch, Kathryn. I know a nice outdoor cafe where Murphy can sit with us. It's nice out today so eating outside will be a treat. I'll drive you to the impound lot when we're finished.'

Neither woman said goodbye.

At the cafe, seated under a red and white striped umbrella, Nikki leaned forward. Her eyes sparkled when she said, 'Tell me everything and don't leave out a word.'

Kathryn talked non-stop for fifteen minutes. 'When it was over, we drove away.'

'Was it worth it, Kathryn? Do you feel vindicated?'

'Oh, yes, Nikki. I'm glad Yoko asked Sid Lee about the others. If she hadn't, I think I would have always wondered. What they did to me, they did to a lot of women. They won't do it ever again, though. I don't suppose anyone heard anything, you know, on the news or the papers?'

'Not that I know of,' Nikki said. 'I don't think it's the kind of thing that will make the news unless they go public. Although, you never know. I can't swear to it but I'll bet you a dollar Charles is tuned into the *LA Times*. By the way, you did good back there.'

'You know, I really would have taken a polygraph test if they wanted to give it.'

'Just the fact that you said you were willing was enough for Jack. Those tests cost money and he really couldn't justify it to his boss. Drink up, Kathryn,' Nikki said holding her wine glass aloft.

They smiled at each other, each busy with her own thoughts.

'Nikki, do you know if Julia—'

'She did it yesterday. She sent them Federal Express from New York. Alexis fixed her up and she drove up there, mailed them and then drove back. She sent them for a ten o'clock delivery. It's two o'clock here on the East Coast and eleven on the West Coast. I think they're probably gazing at their jewels as we speak and wondering how it all went wrong.'

Kathryn smiled and held her glass upward. 'To The Sisterhood! Long may they reign!'

On a balmy spring day just as the first spring flowers bloomed, the Sisterhood met for the second time at Myra Rutledge's McLean estate.

This time, however, the sisters were more vocal with one another, asking about each other's lives and talking about the weather, social events and recipes. The mood was relaxed, not frightening like the first time. Nor was it exhilarating like they thought it would be. It was comfortable, each woman at ease and content in their own skin knowing now their capabilities and using them to the fullest.

Myra banged her gavel on the round table. 'The second meeting of the Sisterhood will now come to order. Are all present and accounted for?'

'Aye,' came the reply.

'Then let's get down to business. In the matter of Kathryn Lucas, was the project successful? Do we have any unfinished business in regard to the project?'

'I think Jack Emery goes under the heading of unfinished business. At the present, I think it's better to let sleeping dogs lie. If the dog should wake and bark, then we can decide what we want to do. I do have one thought where he is concerned,' announced Nikki. 'At some point, he's going to remember the tunnels are under the house. Or, if he doesn't remember on his own, someone might tell him about them. He knows Barbara and I used to play in them when we were children. He knows that because I told him several years ago. I apologize.'

'There's no need to apologize, dear. Six months ago, Charles had the part of the tunnel under the house closed off. Now it looks like the only entrance is from the barn. We used distressed wood and blew cobwebs all over the place. It doesn't look like anyone has been down there for years and years. That particular branch of the tunnel leads to the Danberry Farm. There are no blueprints other than those that belong to this family. I know the Danberrys have a set of prints but they're just for their branch of the tunnels. If Mr Emery's nose starts to twitch, we'll deal with it then.'

Myra looked around the table at the faces she now knew and adored. 'I repeat, was the Kathryn Lucas project successful? How say you all?'

'Aye,' came the reply.

'Kathryn, do you feel avenged?'

'Yes, I do. Thanks to all of you.'

Myra banged the gavel a second time.

'The Kathryn Lucas project is now closed and sealed. We will never speak of it again. Do we all agree?'

'Aye,' came the reply.

Myra banged her gavel a third time. 'It's time to choose our next case. Yoko, do the honors, please.'

Yoko leaned over the table and reached into the shoebox. She withdrew a folded slip of paper and handed it to Myra.

'Sisters, our next case is Alexis Thorne!'

Epilogue

Three days later

'There's something about an early morning breakfast on a terrace that is so special it defies words,' Julia Webster said. 'Look and listen to all the birds. See how pretty all the flowers are in the yard and here on the terrace. I just love beautiful things. I don't mean material things, I mean nature things. Did I tell you all, I ordered a Night Train. My hus . . . the man I'm married to, said it was the stupidest thing I've ever done in my life. I corrected that statement and told him no, the stupidest thing I ever did was to marry him.'

'Atta girl, Julia,' Kathryn said. Julia beamed.

'What's for breakfast?' Alexis queried.

'Fresh melon, freshly squeezed orange juice and *beignets*. A new shop opened in town and the baker is from New Orleans. Charles went to fetch us some. Oh, I hear his car now. We must remember to thank him, sisters. He does love doing things for us.' Myra sighed happily and smiled as Charles opened the small iron gate leading to the terrace.

'Everyone close their eyes! I have a surprise for all of you!' Charles walked over to the table and placed the box of *beignets* in the center of the table. He then placed a copy of the *Tattler* in front of each woman, keeping one for himself. 'You can open your eyes now!'

'Oh myyyy Goddd!' the women said as one.

'As you can see, this sleazy tabloid only mentions the men as Gentleman One, Two and Three. For privacy reasons of course. The doctor all three men consulted had an assistant who spilled the story to the *Tattler* for fifty thousand dollars. She no longer works for the doctor saying 'fifty big ones was a lot better than seven bucks an hour.' That's a direct quote by the way.

'She said, and this is another direct quote, 'One, Two and Three brought their . . . ah . . . bags with them and wanted to know if there was a way to . . . ah . . . reattach them. The contents, not the bags,' Charles guffawed. 'They were told modern medicine hadn't made any inroads in that department. The assistant also said the men were prominent businessmen, cycle enthusiasts and two of them were married and one divorced.

'The men told the physician that it happened on a motorcycle run for a charity benefit. All three of the men think some women on their way to a Harley Davidson show drugged their drinks and did the dirty deed while they were knocked out. One of them recalls hearing a dog bark all night long. As the paper was going to press, no police reports had been filed.

'By the way, the assistant moved to New York the day she received and cashed her check. She is now represented by the William Morris Agency.'

'Oh my goodness,' Myra said.

'Hot damn!' Alexis said.

'No one said anything about my stitches. I do the best stitches in the business,' Julia grumbled. 'And you were all worried they might bleed to death. When I sew 'em up, they're sewed up.'

'This is so exciting,' Yoko babbled. 'We did *that*!' she said pointing to the paper in front of her.

'Yes, we did,' Nikki smiled.

Both of Kathryn's fists shot in the air. 'This is the first time I'm actually glad that modern medicine is lagging behind.'

Isabelle burst out laughing and couldn't stop. Charles thumped her on the back. 'I'm sorry,' she continued to laugh. 'I can just picture them walking into that doctor's office with their nuts in those jars.'

'No, no, Isabelle, I sent them in Ziplock bags in padded envelopes,' Julia said.

'Like when you get goldfish at a pet store! Kathryn, you are truly vindicated,' Isabelle said going off into peals of laughter again.

Charles opened the box on the table. '*Beignets* anyone?'

215